HERE'S HOW IT HAPPENED: LOVESWEPT SENT out a list of themes for the coming months. Things like Men in Uniform, Treasured Tales, Heroes with Tight Butts, etc. While I genuinely wanted to do a book with a theme, and even though the subject of tight, heroic butts is especially dear to my heart, at the time the list arrived I was temporarily brain-dead.

Then shortly afterward, my darling daughter had to cram for an English test, the subject of which was the *Odyssey*.

You see how fate works?

Although Homer's epic poem has always appealed to me—something about the adventure, something about the intrigue, something about a sexy woman who can turn men into pigs—until my recent foray into its depths, I somehow overlooked the romance. Not smart considering what I do for a living.

Literary analysts will tell you that the *Odyssey* is all about testing Odysseus's manhood, but I know they're wrong and now you do too. At its heart, it's the story of a man who fights impossible odds to get back to the woman he loves. And it's the story of a woman who waits. Even when reason tells her that all hope is dead, she waits for the man she loves to come back to her.

Billie Green

WHAT ARE *LOVESWEPT* ROMANCES?

They are stories of true romance and touching emotion. We believe those two very important ingredients are constants in our highly sensual and very believable stories in the LOVESWEPT line. Our goal is to give you, the reader, stories of consistently high quality that may sometimes make you laugh, sometimes make you cry, but are always fresh and creative and contain many delightful surprises within their pages.

Most romance fans read an enormous number of books. Those they truly love, they keep. Others may be traded with friends and soon forgotten. We hope that each LOVESWEPT romance will be a treasure—a "keeper." We will always try to publish

LOVE STORIES YOU'LL NEVER FORGET
BY AUTHORS YOU'LL ALWAYS REMEMBER

The Editors

BABY, COME BACK

BILLIE GREEN

BANTAM BOOKS

NEW YORK · TORONTO · LONDON · SYDNEY · AUCKLAND

BABY, COME BACK

A Bantam Book / January 1994

ISBN 0-553-44333-X

Published simultaneously in the United States and Canada

Bantam Books are published by Bantam Books, a division of Bantam Doubleday Dell Publishing Group, Inc. Its trademark, consisting of the words
"Bantam Books" and the portrayal of a rooster, is Registered in U.S. Patent
and Trademark Office and in other countries. Marca Registrada. Bantam
Books, 1540 Broadway, New York, New York 10036.

PRINTED IN THE UNITED STATES OF AMERICA

OPM   0 9 8 7 6 5 4 3 2 1

To Jeanie,
for not giving up on me just because I'm a squirrel, and for saving my butt.

PROLOGUE

Keeping well to the center of the narrow, worn path, David turned another corner. In the maze there was always another corner, always another passage that inevitably looped around to lead him back the way he came.

His feet were encased in iron boots, so that each step was awkward and laboriously slow. His gaze, watchful, cautious, moved unceasingly from side to side. The thick thornbushes that lined the sides of the labyrinth sometimes came alive, reaching out to tear at his body, and he was never able to move fast enough to get out of harm's way.

God, he was tired. Tired of dragging his feet forward, tired of fighting the grasping thorns. But he couldn't stop. He couldn't take time to rest. Something inside him forced him to keep going, forced him to take one more sluggish step. Then another and another.

Around the next corner he came to a place he recognized. He had passed this way before. Many times.

This time, however, something was different. Directly ahead, there was an opening in the thick hedge. Sunlight streamed through the gap, making a spot of misty brightness in the gloom.

Was it another trick? If he drew nearer the opening, would the hateful branches use the opportunity to rip at him again?

David had to take the chance. The brightness was irresistible. He had to get closer.

Dragging his feet forward, he tripped several times in his haste to reach the breach in the never-ending green wall, but at last he was there.

He glanced around, all his senses alert as he waited for the trap to be sprung. When nothing happened, he leaned closer, slowly, carefully, and looked through.

On the other side of the hedge was a world of wonder. Green was a different color there. The green of spring, the green of renewal. There were glorious flowers on the other side, bright skies, and singing birds.

On the other side of the hedge was life.

On the other side was Kathy.

She stood in an open field, her body bathed with gentle light, and as David watched she turned her head and looked directly at him.

His heart began to beat with a jarring force as he pushed forward into the small gap, indifferent to the barbs that went deep into his chest and arms, unmindful of the thorns that ripped at his face, turning it into a bloody mess.

Moving furiously, he fought the hedge. He had to get to her. He had to let her know—

"He's coming around. . . . Help me hold him down! Gabriella, have the hypodermic ready. The next few minutes are going to be painful as hell."

Although the voice came from a great distance, its presence was intrusive, disturbing. Clenching his teeth, he blocked it out. He couldn't let it distract him. He couldn't afford to acknowledge the voice's connection with reality. He had to focus all his energy and attention on his battle with the crucifying branches.

He was halfway through now. If only he could pull his legs free, he would be on the other side. He would be in the world where Kathy was.

Oh God, something was happening.

Glancing around frantically, he groaned as darkness began to fall over him. The branches were pulling him back. The hedge was starting to close around him, blocking the sun, sealing off the way back to Kathy.

He could still see her through the last remaining gap, but she was in shadow now, her face twisted with fear as she took a slow step backward.

Sweet Jesus, she couldn't see him. She was walking away. Kathy was leaving!

He couldn't lose her again. He couldn't. He had to

find a way to stop her, to make her understand that he was here, that he was doing everything he could to get to her.

Pushing the branches away from his face, he screamed her name. Again and again he screamed. But the sound was all wrong. Her name was lost, twisted by the nightmare hedge, and only harsh, rasping sounds came from his throat.

Then, as though some remnant of the pitiful noise reached her, she looked back, tilting her head slightly as she strained to see.

An instant later her eyes grew wide with recognition. She saw him! She was coming back.

But it was too late. Already the dark, stagnant green had closed, sealing him off.

Closing his eyes, David moaned in an agony of frustration and pain. If only he had fought harder, if only he had been able to talk to her, if only—

It was all gone. The world of brightness and wonder was gone.

Kathy was gone.

And David was back in the maze alone.

"So you're finally going to wake up," the voice of reality said as David opened his eyes.

ONE

"Are you going all the way to Dallas?"

The seat next to David Moore was empty, so he looked farther afield to find the source of the question. Seated across the aisle was a young woman who had gotten on the bus at the last stop. Brassy red curls framed a face that would have been attractive had it not been hidden under a heavy layer of makeup. She was sitting sideways, her feet propped up in the seat beside her as she studied David with undisguised interest.

For the past hour he had been held in thrall by the changing mosaic of green that lined the highway, but he didn't mind the interruption. Listening to a Texas accent was as pleasing to him as watching a Texas spring.

"All the way to Dallas," he confirmed.

As though something about his voice intrigued

her, the woman tilted her head to the side and smiled. "Paying a visit to the big city? Looking for work?"

"Going home," he said softly.

"You say that kind of sad. Has it been a long time since you've seen your family?"

He nodded once, slowly. "Six years." The words were barely audible. "Yes, it's been a long time."

If one said the words quickly, if one didn't give them any serious thought, six years didn't sound like so much. But when a man had counted off every interminable minute of those six years, it was a long time. A long, long time.

Six years ago time hadn't been all that important to David. At thirty-two, he had been a professor of economics at a small, prestigious university in Dallas. He had a beautiful wife and the world's brightest ten-month-old baby boy. His personal life was perfect, his professional life secure. He was cocky back then, smug, certain that he had all the time in the world. But that was six years ago.

Sweet heaven, *six years*.

David closed his eyes, his body tense as he fought traces of distant fear, echoes of desperation, memories of soul-shattering loneliness.

It was *over*. He had to let it go. Because as long as any fragment of the nightmare remained, as long as it still had the power to shake him, he wasn't yet free.

"I sure hope DeeDee remembers she was supposed to pick me up."

After glancing again at the redhead across the aisle, David sat up straighter and looked around. The bus was already pulling into the station. He had been lost in his thoughts for over an hour.

"My friend DeeDee is coming to pick me up," the woman explained. "At least she's supposed to. I told her not to go out and party last night because when she drinks, her brain is somewhere else for a couple of days."

When the bus came to a complete stop, she rose to her feet and met his eyes. "DeeDee is really a dead loss as a friend," she confided, "but when someone needs you, what are you gonna do?"

Giving her an understanding smile, David picked up a small canvas bag and followed the handful of passengers off the bus. While the others huddled, waiting for their luggage, he stood apart from them, glancing around, trying to get his bearings.

"Is someone coming to pick you up?"

It was the redhead again. She had moved to stand beside him, a cosmetics case in one hand and a vinyl garment bag thrown casually over her shoulder.

"No." He shook his head slowly. "My— No one knows I'm here."

She smiled, her black-lined eyes flirting openly again. "So you're just going to show up and surprise them? How fun. They'll like that. Do you need a ride? DeeDee won't mind. You don't mind, do you, DeeDee?" she said to a young blond woman who was approaching as fast as her skintight skirt would allow.

"Kerry, you silly, silly slug. You didn't tell me there would be so much traffic on this side of town," the newcomer scolded in a voice that carried across the entire area. "And wouldn't you know, the radio in John's old clunker picked today to commit suicide. I can't drive without music. I really can't. I think it's something in my genes. I'm not lying. I was born with it. My mother is always telling me how, when I was little, I would—"

"*DeeDee*, for once in your life will you stop talking long enough to listen? I'm trying to ask you—"

"That's all right," David said, his voice low and husky. "I can make my own way home. But I appreciate the offer," he added as he began to move away.

"Kerry, Kerry, Kerry. Who was *that*?"

Already halfway across the room, David chuckled at the urgency in the blonde's high-pitched voice.

"Did you find him on the bus?" she continued. "Those sleepy eyes. That voice. Whiskey and sex. Didn't his voice sound like whiskey and sex to you? It gave me the shivers. I mean, it was a real, physical thing. Why didn't you offer him a ride?"

"You dimwit," the redhead said in a voice rich with disgust. "I ought to—"

The rest of her threat was lost as David pushed open a door and walked out into the open air.

Starting down the sidewalk, he began to absorb the feel of the city. David had passed through a lot of places on his way back, but Dallas was home.

Kathy was here, and that made it home.

As the sounds and smells reached him he let his mind slide into memories that reached much further back than six years. Good memories. Safe memories.

Like the day he met Kathy.

As usual, David had been late for a class. Pre-occupied with the charts and graphs he would use in the morning session, he had walked straight into her.

Books and papers flew in a dozen different directions, and when he and his victim both dropped to their knees in an attempt to sort out the mess, he listened for a moment to the blue velvet sound of her voice before interrupting her apology.

"It was my fault. I wasn't watching where I was going. I never do," he added without repentance.

When she raised her eyes to his, he drew back his head in what felt like shock.

The ash-blond hair that curled gently around her face was short and baby soft, providing a frame for features that had a fine delicacy to them. An aura of gentle elegance and subdued intelligence surrounded her, calling to mind the women who had lived in the south at the turn of the century.

As she stared at him in return her lips curved ever so slightly in a smile. The look in her green eyes were distracted, as though her thoughts were perpetually elsewhere.

She was lovely. Absolutely lovely.

But it wasn't her beauty that so firmly captured his attention. There were plenty of beautiful women on campus, and being human, David had noticed them all. But like pieces of fine art, they were designed to be enjoyed from a distance.

This woman was different. Like a spring day, she was a delight to all the senses. A phenomenon. An event to be intimately experienced. And like that perfect day in spring, she made a man want to ditch work and spend his time in frivolous, delirious pleasure.

Tilting his head back, David frowned at her in concentration. "Do I know you? I'm sure I've seen you. Are you one of my students?"

"I was. For a little while."

"You dropped my class? Why?" he asked with characteristic bluntness. "What have you got against economics?"

"Nothing . . . that is—" The distant, wistful smile was again playing across her lips. "I'm afraid I switched to Professor Yates's class."

"Yates? You've got to be kidding." David quickly scooped up the rest of his things and rose to his feet, studying her with astonishment. "You actually prefer Boo Yates to me? Are you using his class to catch up on your sleep?"

It was strange. Although David could have sworn she was laughing, the dancing light in her green eyes was the only detectable sign of amusement.

"You intrigue me, young lady," he said, using his best and most pompous professor voice. "If I had more time, I would definitely get to the bottom of this."

But David hadn't had more time, so he had reluctantly walked away from her. For the rest of the day, at unexpected times and with vivid clarity, that lovely, gentle face had drifted through his mind, scattering his thoughts, playing hell with his concentration.

That same evening when his front doorbell rang, he was sitting in his study, staring out the window, still thinking of her.

When he found the object of his thoughts on his doorstep, David frowned as he rubbed his chin. Then, without greeting or preamble, he said, "Since it's inconceivable that you think Yates is a better educator, you must have changed your schedule. You tried desperately to switch to another of my classes, but because I'm so popular, they were all filled. Is that how it happened?"

Although she neither confirmed nor denied his theory, once again the dancing sparks appeared in her eyes.

He leaned his shoulder against the door, perfectly willing to be fascinated by her. "Now why are you laughing?"

"I'm not laughing."

"Not on the outside, but inside you're giggling like crazy. At my expense, I'm afraid. Why?"

"You're vain," she explained, her lower lip quivering with contained amusement.

"Anyone with a good mind is vain. It comes with the territory. So if you came all the way here to tell me that, you wasted your time. I already knew."

This time she had to bite her lip to keep from laughing. After clearing her throat, she said, "I came to see if my English-lit paper got mixed up with your things."

Stepping back, he motioned her inside. "Yes, I have it. And based on that paper, I think I would allow you a little vanity of your own."

"You read my—" She stopped walking and glanced at him. "Only a little?"

"You're young yet. Give it time." He frowned as a sudden thought struck him. "How young?"

"Twenty-one."

"Good," he said succinctly, then turned to lead the way to his study.

David's conscience might have bothered him a little if she had been as young as she appeared. Her youth wouldn't have stopped him, but he might have had a few qualms to overcome. Because the moment he opened the door and found her there, it had all became clear. David had seen his future.

She moved across the room and stood gazing out the same window he had been staring out of earlier. He saw the sunlight settling on her, picking out bits of platinum in her hair, and he had wondered if when he came to know what went on behind those misty green eyes, he would love her as much as he did at that moment.

Now, walking down a busy street in Dallas, David remembered that day and knew he hadn't loved Kathy as much when he came to know her better. He had loved her more. More than he had ever dreamed was possible.

Reaching in his pocket, he pulled out a handful of change and stared at it for a moment. His destination was the far north side of the city. It was going to be a long walk.

As he passed a small bookstore his movement, reflected in the dusty display window, caught his eye. He stopped walking and turned to examine his own see-through image.

Sun-darkened skin. Thick brown hair, long enough to cover the collar of his cotton shirt. Gold-brown eyes that drooped slightly at the outer corners. Broad shoulders that didn't match his tall, too lean frame.

Where David had been, mirrors weren't that common. He had rarely had the chance to look at his own face, to study the changes six years had wrought. After staring for a while, he reached up to run the tips of two fingers across the high cheek-bones and down the hard line of his jaw, watching as his reflection mimicked the action.

An instant later cold sweat broke out on his upper lip and forehead. His hands trembled and his heart pounded with wild, jarring thuds. Panic reached out and gripped him by the throat with a force that almost lifted him off his feet.

The acute attacks of anxiety weren't new. They struck at odd times and without warning. One minute David would be fine, the next he suddenly would be overcome by the need to run and keep on running.

Turning abruptly away from the window, he clenched his teeth and drew a rough hand across his face. He pulled in a deep, unsteady breath as he searched for calm. Another breath, then another and another, until the riot within him finally began to subside.

When he started walking again, David's steps were slower, less confident. He needed decent clothes. Transportation. A little cash in his pocket. He had to—

Just then a delivery truck rumbled to a stop beside him. The driver opened the door and whistled through his teeth as he walked around to the back of the vehicle.

Moving a step closer, David studied the fading black letters on the door of the truck.

SEUTER'S SAV-MORE
Discount Building Supplies

Ralph Seuter.

The owner of the thirty-odd Seuter's Sav-Mores that were spread across north Texas was a cranky old man with more money than couth. He was also the best friend David had in the world.

Reveling in the eccentric, Ralph had a routine that hadn't varied in thirty years. He left his enormous west Dallas estate at five in the morning and sat for three hours at a truck stop while he drank coffee with a lot of other cranky old men, all dressed as badly as he was. From there he went to his office at Sav-More headquarters. At eleven-thirty, not one minute before or one minute after, he left the office and drove across town to Flora's Diner, a café that had been serving chicken fried steak with greasy gravy in the same disreputable building since the Great Depression. The rest of Ralph's workday was spent harassing the managers of the five Sav-Mores in the Dallas-Fort Worth area.

Flora's Diner was only two blocks from where David stood now. If he hurried, he would be able to catch Ralph at exactly the right time, after the old man's hunger had been appeased and before indigestion set in.

Turning right at the next corner, David smiled, pulling up a mental picture of the man who had been his first employer.

David had been just sixteen when he took a part-time job at one of the suburban Sav-Mores to help supplement his grandmother's small pension. It was during Ralph's daily visits to the lumber-yard that David had come to know and like the older man.

The following year, after his grandmother died and Ralph gave his young employee a home, David had come to love him.

It was Ralph who finished the job of raising David. He bought David his first car, then made him work his butt off to pay for his first speeding ticket. He boasted to all his friends when David won a coveted scholarship, then dragged David off the campus by his shirt collar when he partied too long and slept through an important exam.

Praising and censuring with the same thunderous vigor, Ralph had taught David about being a man.

It was on the night before David's wedding, as

he was leaving for a night of carousing with his friends, that Ralph had given his protégé one last piece of parental counsel.

"I figure you're as close to a son as I'll ever have," Ralph told him. "I know you're twenty-nine and you think because you've spent most of your life in schools, that makes you one sharp son of a bitch, but you've still got a few things to learn, the kind of things they don't teach at college."

"Is this a father-son talk?" David asked, grinning. "Are you going to tell me about the birds and bees now?"

The older man gave a short bark of laughter. "Hell, boy, you know more about sex than I do, or ever want to, for that matter. Some things ought to be left to instinct. No, I'm talking about life now. And I know a damn sight more about living than you do, because I've been doing it a damn sight longer."

Ralph paused, reaching up to rub his wide, square jaw. "You've been through a lot in your life, losing your parents when you were just a little kid, then having your granny kick off before you got good and grown. But it seems to me that none of that stuff put a real dent in you. You've still got your original coat of paint."

David, used to Ralph's bluntness, chuckled. "Don't be so subtle. Just come right out and say I'm shallow."

But Ralph would not be put off by David's teasing. He had a point to make and he was not going to give up until he made it.

"I don't mean you didn't feel it," he continued. "I was there when your granny died and I know how it hurt you. But young people bounce back pretty easy. I just want you to know it's not always going to be that way. Someday something will happen that will dig some character lines in your face, put some gray in your hair."

David, eager to get to his bachelor party, gave Ralph an affectionate punch in the arm. "Look, you old geezer, you've been my father, my mother, my boss, and my conscience since I was seventeen years old. If I don't have what I need to survive in this world, it sure as hell won't be your fault."

The older man studied David's face for a moment. "You remember that Roman god you told me about, the one who worked with metal? I always liked that fellow. Because he was about life. Real life. Sooner or later that guy catches up with all of us. It's going to happen to you, too, son. You can make book on it. And when you've been through his fire, you'll either come out a useless pile of ashes or tempered steel, stronger than you ever were before. I just want you to be prepared for it. Don't let it ruin you, son. Use it."

Now, as he spotted the small dingy café down

the street, David wondered if Ralph still remembered those words, if he ever considered their irony.

Just before he reached the café's entrance, the door opened and a large man wearing a shabby brown suit walked out. He moved past David without looking at him and made his way to a battered '69 Ford.

"Ralph?"

The older man turned and looked at him, annoyance showing in the lines around his mouth and eyes.

"It happened just the way you told me it would," David said in the perpetual husky whisper that was his voice. "Vulcan finally caught up with me." His lips twisted in a rueful smile. "I was prepared for the forge, but you didn't tell me I'd have to take a turn on his anvil as well."

All the color drained from the old man's face, leaving it gray and slack as he took an awkward step back and bumped into the car door.

Turning his head to the side, he stared at David with narrowed eyes. *"Who the hell are you?"*

TWO

As David watched the old man reached up to rake an unsteady hand across his face. When Ralph's knees buckled, David leapt forward and grasped him around the waist, supporting him as he opened the car door and helped him inside.

Moving around the car, David slid into the passenger seat and leaned across to loosen Ralph's tie and shirt collar.

"You old geezer," he scolded roughly as he worked. "Calm down. There's no need to get your bowels in an uproar. Isn't that what you always used to say? You ought to think about taking your own advice once in a while."

Ralph groaned, moving his head uneasily. "Back off. Don't crowd me."

The older man's voice was stronger now and as gruff as always, but he still looked pale. Opening his eyes, he blinked several times, as though he were trying to bring his eyes into focus.

"How do you know those things?" he rasped out. "That he always called me old geezer, that I used to tell him not to get his bowels in an uproar? And that stuff you said about Vulcan's forge. How could you—"

He broke off and suddenly sat up straighter, his gaze growing avid. "Were you with David? Were you with my boy when he died?"

My boy. David swallowed past the lump in his throat. The old man really loved him. This was turning out to be more difficult than he had imagined.

Glancing away, David drew in a slow breath and cleared his throat. "He didn't die, Ralph," he said in a slow, rasping whisper.

A long tense silence followed his statement, then Ralph turned in the seat and began grappling with the door handle beside him. "I don't know what you're trying to pull," he muttered, "but you picked the wrong sucker. You should have checked out your facts. David Moore left six years ago to—"

Reaching across him, David pulled Ralph's hand away from the handle. "He left to attend a conference in Gamarra," he finished for him, "where a bunch of brains were going to get together and try to solve all of that miserable little country's problems."

When David had been asked to participate in the week-long conference in the small Central American country, both he and Kathy had been enthusiastic. It was a great honor to have been invited. Although he didn't like the idea of being separated from his wife and son, even for a week, the chance of exchanging ideas with people he had only read about was exciting, the opportunity of a lifetime.

"I'll miss you like crazy," Kathy had told him, "but you have to go. Just make sure you don't eat any strange food . . . or sleep in any strange beds."

Now, remembering her words, David gave a hoarse laugh. He had slept in some pretty strange beds, but not the kind Kathy had been talking about.

"You owe me an explanation," Ralph said, rallying again to pull David back to the present. "If you had read any of the newspapers from back then, you'd know that David was taken hostage when—"

"The conference was in its second day when the revolution broke out," David continued. "And before the government could even begin evacuating foreigners, eight men were taken hostage by the rebel forces." He paused and his voice grew thick and even more husky. "All were academics, not a single one of them prepared to be caught up in a war."

"And two years later the bastards killed them all," Ralph said. "David has been dead for four years. We saw the *pictures*. They were lying in a pile . . . like they were nothing, like they were yesterday's trash. A bloody, ungodly mess." He turned his head away. "Four years and I can still see those pictures when I close my eyes."

David had seen the photographs as well. His captors had taken delight in showing them to him, letting him know that because everyone now believed he was dead, there was no hope of rescue.

"His face was gone," Ralph whispered. "I have nightmares when I think of what they did to him, how much pain he must have endured before he died."

"Don't think about it." David's voice was hard, his muscles tense. "It accomplishes nothing."

Sucking in a harsh breath, he fought to push the memories away. He couldn't be distracted by them now. He needed to maintain control.

"Ralph," he said slowly, "I want you to think about something else instead. Suppose in that bloody, ungodly mess, in that pile of dead bodies, one man was still alive . . . barely. Suppose they took him to someone who could patch him up. Suppose . . ."

The word faded as, against his will, David remembered a man from the past, a nameless, merciless doctor.

"*I did the best I could. If I'd had a photograph to work from, maybe I could have put you back the way you were. Maybe. It was like working a blood-soaked jigsaw puzzle. They told me to make you look human again, and that's what I did. Besides, it's not such a bad face.*"

Not a bad face, David thought now, but not his.

He glanced at Ralph and found that the old man was leaning toward him, studying the terrain of his face with narrowed, suspicious eyes.

"What are you trying to say?" Ralph leaned closer. "And where the hell did you get eyes that color?"

David laughed. "I didn't steal them, you old—" He broke off when his friend slumped back against the seat. "Take it easy. You shouldn't get so excited. It's bad for your blood pressure. Considering all the garbage you eat, you should have been dead years ago."

The old man closed his eyes. "The anvil. You . . . David?" The word was weak, barely audible.

"Yes, it's me."

"But your face . . . your voice."

Another flash of memory. A heavy, brown boot coming toward David's face in a vicious kick. Pain that seemed to go on forever.

Clenching his fists, he took in several shallow

breaths. He had to stop this. He didn't have time to deal with the old panic.

"There was some damage done to my larynx. Permanent damage." He shrugged his shoulders. "You get used to it."

It was the last beating that had ruined his voice, but it was also the last beating that had freed him. His captors, assuming he was too weak to move, had left him unguarded for too long. David had crawled into the jungle and kept crawling until he passed out.

When he regained consciousness he was in a dingy little room, being cared for by a rural doctor and his family. For a while David couldn't remember how he came to be there. He didn't know why he was in pain or why he couldn't talk. But as the days passed and he began to heal, it all came back to him. Everything.

And that was when David began making plans to get home, as quickly and with as little fuss as possible.

"I didn't want strangers telling you and Kathy about me," he told Ralph now. "That's why I didn't go to the American embassy. I had to sneak across a few borders, but I still think I did the right thing. After six years I couldn't stand the idea of being stuck down there with a lot of grim-faced government types giving me the third degree. I had to get home."

After a brief, tense pause he glanced at the man beside him. "Tell me what's been happening with Kathy."

Ralph shifted in his seat and ran an unsteady hand through his thin hair. "She goes by Kate now."

"That doesn't tell me any—" He broke off. "Why would she do that?"

"You were the only one who ever called her Kathy. To everyone else she was always Katherine, but she said if she was going to succeed in business, she needed a name that sounded stronger, more practical."

David shook his head, frowning in confusion. "I don't understand. What business?"

Ralph shrugged. "Insurance money doesn't last forever."

"But her parents—"

"They would have supported her. So would I. But she wouldn't allow it. She said everything had changed and she had to change too. She had to grow up and make her own way in the world. I have to admit, she's doing a pretty damn good job of it."

David felt suddenly claustrophobic. He couldn't take in what Ralph was saying. It didn't make sense. Kathy. Sweet, vulnerable Kathy. A business-woman?

When he saw that Ralph was watching him

closely, he rearranged his features, hiding the riotous unease that was once again trying to take control.

"Tell me about my boy, Ralph."

Instantly the older man's face lit up, his mouth curving in an outright grin. "Ben's all right. A genuine ring-tailed tooter." The grin slid away abruptly and his eyes grew cloudy with sadness. "I'm sorry you weren't there to see him grow, son. Those people, did they—"

David shook his head emphatically. "That's all in the past, not worth talking about. I need to think about the future now."

"Well hell, boy. You can't just show up, looking like someone else, sounding like someone else, and say it's not worth talking about. If you don't want to tell me what they did to you, at least explain why they held on to you. I've heard about French soldiers being released from Cambodia after twenty years, and the Russians held World War Two prisoners even longer than that. I know it happens, but why?"

"Damned if I know." David's lips twisted in a crooked smile. "Maybe they just didn't know how to quit. Maybe when the old regime regained power and their original objective lost meaning, they continued out of habit. Why did they keep me alive, patch me up, and then go on trying to kill me?" He shook his head. "I don't know and I honestly don't care. Now, are you going to help me or not?"

"That's a stupid question. Of course I'll help. What do you need?"

"What every son needs from his father, even a latter-day father." Grinning, he held out his hand. "Can I have some cash and the keys to the car, Dad?"

When Ralph laughed, David leaned back in the seat and drew in a slow breath. It was finally going to happen. After six years of thinking about it, six years of dreaming about it, it was finally going to happen.

"I'm going home, Ralph," he whispered. "I'm finally going home."

THREE

Kate Moore sat at the small wooden table in the kitchen, her chin resting in one palm as she stared fixedly at the report in front of her.

Several feet away, at the kitchen counter, a woman in her midfifties stood with her back to the room as she pounded away at a cut of pork. Veda Johnson had been Kate's housekeeper, cook, and resident critic for the past three years.

" . . . ink smears on the table, paper clips all over the floor. And who has to clean it all up? Tell me that. You have a perfectly good office down the hall. Your computer's in there. Your files and charts and high-finance doohickeys. Why do you have to work in here all the time, making messes and getting in my way?"

"It's my house," Kate said. "I can work anywhere I want to." She raised her head to send the older woman an annoyed look. "Isn't that meat tender yet?"

"I like hitting it," Veda said without pausing in her destruction. "I pretend it's my ex-husband."

Kate sputtered with laughter. "I should have known. Which of your many men are we having for dinner tonight? The one you caught rolling around on the dirty laundry with your cousin the slut, or the one who emptied your bank account and moved to New Zealand?"

"Neither." Veda held up the battered piece of pork, an expression of satisfaction settling across her features. "This is Trip."

Trip was short for triple because he happened to be the third L. D. LaSalle in his family. Veda had married him on her fifteenth birthday and left him before she turned sixteen.

"Trip LaSalle had two sides to him," Veda said, staring at the tenderloin that she still held aloft. "One side was better than good, and the other side was worse than bad, but I loved him more than all the others put together. That's why I still hate him after all these years. It's not good to love a man too much."

Switching her attention back to her work, Kate muttered, "If you feel like that, why do you keep hounding me to get married?"

"Because you have a boring life." Veda moved closer, shaking a wooden mallet at Kate to emphasize her point. "The most exciting thing that's happened around here in months was when your computer system broke down and you had to decide what kind you were going to buy to replace it." She rolled her eyes. "Lord, give me strength. *Boring.* It doesn't make any kind of sense. There are half a dozen men who would marry you anytime you say the word."

"You hate my men friends," Kate reminded her as she began separating her work into three small piles.

"Bunch of God-blessed wienies," Veda muttered. "It beats me how you always end up with wusses. It's like you've got a sign on your forehead, 'Real men need not apply.'" She made a short sound of contempt. "Lately I've been thinking that maybe that's the way you want it. Dull, dull, and more dull. I bet you'd choke on your tongue if one of your powder puffs ever put a serious move on you."

"I suppose all the men you married were 'real men.' Pardon me if I'm not impressed. If you're so interested in having a wedding, have another of your own." Pushing back her chair, she went to the refrigerator and pulled out a bottle of mineral water. "You've done it so often, I'm surprised they don't use a Magic Slate for the marriage license. It would sure save the county a lot of paperwork."

"Very funny." Veda dropped the mangled pork

in a bowl of marinade, then turned back to Kate, her hands on her hips. "Since we're arguing anyway, didn't you tell me you would hire someone to build new shelves in the pantry by the end of last week? Well, where is he, huh? Where is he? If I get killed by a falling jar of pickles, you'll be sorry."

"No, I won't," Kate told her calmly. "I'll celebrate. And I'll make sure they bury you in that green dress. The one that makes you look like broccoli that's been in the refrigerator too long."

Regaining her seat at the table, she added, "The agency is sending over a couple of men today for me to interview. You can choose the one you like . . . because we both know this isn't about shelves. You simply have some kind of perverted passion for men with tool belts, tattoos, and visible butt cleavage."

"At least I know what I'm looking at and why I'm looking at it. I bet you don't even remember the last time you set eyes on some naked male buns." The older woman raised one brow in speculation. "Or has Junior been dropping his drawers for you?"

The thought of Junior Thibideaux, a man who probably slept in a three-piece suit, exposing his bare posterior made Kate burst out laughing.

"Smart-ass," she said, shaking her head.

"Bitch," the housekeeper replied, smiling against her will as she took off her apron. "I'm going to the store for fresh greens. They probably won't have that fancy lettuce you like. You and your dinner guest will just have to make do with plain old iceberg."

"That'll show me."

"Screw you, Kate Moore," Veda muttered as she picked up her purse and stalked out of the room.

Chuckling, Kate turned to glance out the window. Although she liked annoying Veda, the real reason Kate worked in the kitchen was so that she could keep a discreet eye on her seven-year-old son.

Kate was very careful to put forth the image of a calm, efficient mother. She didn't want Ben stifled by her secret fears. But in reality, she was a genuine nervous Nellie, the kind of mother who panicked every time her child was out of her sight. Kate had lost too much. She couldn't bear the thought of losing Ben as well.

Now, as her gaze moved across the backyard, she felt the familiar anxiety begin to nudge at her. Where was he?

Leaving her work, she walked out the backdoor and almost immediately spotted his red shirt among the lower branches of an ancient cedar tree. Just looking at the cedar made her itch, but its prickly needles never seemed to bother Ben. He was probably drafting changes on the treehouse he had been planning to build off and on for the past six months.

As she felt the tension ease away she gave a soft laugh, amused now by her own foolishness. Ben was fine. Better than fine. The world's best kid. Superstar of sons.

That she could have produced and single-handedly raised such a wonderful boy constantly amazed Kate. Not that there hadn't been mistakes. She had made plenty of them, especially in the beginning, but fortunately, Ben seemed impervious to her screwups. No traumas. Not a single neurosis. Just a top-notch, lord-of-all-he-surveyed kid.

Instead of returning to the kitchen, she moved to sit in the wooden swing that was suspended from the limb of a huge oak and began rocking gently back and forth.

Kate had been a widow for four years and alone for six.

Six years. A lifetime.

Veda had told her more than once that she was doing Ben an injustice by refusing to provide him with a father. Her parents assumed that every man she dated was a candidate for marriage. Even Ralph had begun to hint that it might not hurt if she started thinking about settling down.

But Kate wasn't sure she would ever marry again. There was no way it could ever be like it was with David. She could never love anyone the way she had loved David. Even if it were possible, Kate wouldn't allow it to happen.

Her opinionated housekeeper had been right about one thing. That kind of love hurt too much when you lost it.

As she sat staring at the house, her beautifully, expensively renovated house, she suddenly saw it as it had been eight years ago.

Back then she had been an inexperienced girl of twenty-two, eager to please, eager for happiness, eager for David. David, on the other hand, had been twenty-nine. Older and wiser. Totally confident. Completely in love.

On that particular day, two weeks before their wedding, they were lost. David was always getting lost and he always vehemently denied being lost. Exploring new venues, was the way he put it.

They had spotted the house at the same time. The small For Sale sign nailed to the weed-choked front fence looked almost as old as the house. To Kathy the house was a setting for a ghost story or a sad love song. But David hadn't seen it that way. He looked beyond the sagging porch and boarded-up windows and saw a home. Their home. Something different. Something uniquely their own.

When they returned from their honeymoon, although repairs were under way, the house was barely fit to live in. But live in it they did. They lived in it and loved in it and tried to get a marriage going in the midst of painters and plumbers and carpenters.

One night, as they lay together on the floor in front of the fireplace in the room that would someday be their bedroom, David sat up abruptly and looked down at her.

"Do you know what this is?" he asked, indicating the object in his right hand.

Kathy examined his face, a dear face, a face that made her smile just by looking at it. Even though her husband could never be described as handsome, he drew people to him, using nothing more than a cocky smile and a twinkle in his eyes.

David's eyes had fascinated her from the very beginning. They should have been brown. At least that was Kathy's theory. God started out making them brown but got distracted by something else for a moment. So instead of brown, his eyes were golden. Not yellow like a cat. Golden. Like honey. Like aged whiskey. Like sunshine seen through a smoky haze.

At this particular moment his smoky-gold eyes weren't gleaming. They were sober, and his brow was creased with concentration.

Kathy felt a lecture coming on. At times like these her husband not only looked like an economics professor, he sounded like one as well.

"Do you know what this is?" he repeated.

Lowering her gaze, she studied the object in his hand. "A champagne cork?"

"Wrong. It's a champagne cork."

An economics professor who, at the moment, was one step to the left of sober.

"But you have to think beyond what you see," he went on. "This represents tonight. Everything about tonight. Eating cold roasted chicken with our fingers, drinking champagne out of the juice glasses the dean gave us, making love on a canvas that smells like sawdust and paint."

She leaned forward, looking more closely. "All that's in that little thing?"

"You bet your sweet buns it is. And more. Much, much more. This piece of compressed cork is the memory of tonight. And since memories last as long as you want them to, this"— he raised his hand, holding the cork high— "is forever." He cut his eyes toward her. "Follow me?"

"Anywhere," she murmured with a loving smile.

"Good." Rising to his feet, he pulled her up and began dragging her out of the room.

"Where are we going?"

"We're going to hide our forever so no one can steal it from us."

In the backyard, she walked behind him, both of them naked as the day they were born, while he tramped around and looked through the ragged shrubbery, searching out secluded spots in their new-old backyard.

Eventually he stopped in front of the oak tree. After walking around it several times, he reached up and began to clear the leaves out of a knothole that was several inches above her head.

"This'll do just fine." He turned to her and held out the cork. "Okay, now you have to kiss it."

She laughed and did as she was told.

"Now you have to kiss me . . . and this time use some tongue."

Again she did as she was told.

Fifteen minutes later David's breathing was erratic and his hands roamed restlessly over her naked back, pressing her closer. "Why didn't we bring a blanket?" he whispered hoarsely against her lips. "Making love in the backyard is a great idea—like all my ideas—but we should have brought a blanket."

"We didn't come out here to make love." She moved against him, bringing a groan from deep in his throat. "We came out here to hide our forever."

"That's no excuse." After giving her one last kiss, one last loving stroke, he pulled back and glanced up at the knothole. Then he kissed the cork in the exact spot her lips had touched earlier.

And as she watched, his expression changed, growing serious, intense. "This is forever, Kathy," he whispered, his voice rough with emotion as he stared into her eyes. "You and me. Forever."

"Forever," Kathy repeated then.

"Forever," Kate whispered now.

It hadn't been forever. It wasn't even two years later that he went away from her.

And then he died.

Kate turned slightly in the swing and raised her head until she located the knothole, once again filled with dead leaves. Years and years of dead leaves.

A soft shiver went through her and she closed her eyes, silently fighting the shattering sadness, the soul-deep loneliness.

I can't do this again, she told herself. She couldn't let the feelings overwhelm her. If Veda came back and found her sitting in a swing, crying for the past, she would give Kate hell. The older woman would nag and lecture and forecast doom, telling Kate that if she didn't get a man, all her female parts would dry up and fall out.

Veda had a way with words.

"Gotta get me a man," Kate said aloud, tilting way back in the swing.

When she opened her eyes, a man was standing directly behind her.

For a moment Kate stayed as she was, looking at him upside down, wondering if he was real. When she realized what she was doing, she hastily stood up and turned to face him.

The man in her backyard was a stranger. A stranger with a face that looked like it had been chiseled from the side of a mountain. It was strong and ruggedly attractive, intimidating in its maleness. He was tall and his shoulders were broad. But as though he had been ill recently, his height and the breadth of his shoulders didn't match the rest of his lean body. His hair was longer than what was currently fashionable, and he wore a plain blue cotton shirt. Both hands were tucked into the back pockets of his tight-fitting jeans.

He didn't move and he didn't speak. He simply stood on the opposite side of the swing and stared at her. It wasn't a casual stare. The look was penetrating and almost fierce in its intensity, causing Kate to take a small step backward in involuntary reaction.

A moment later, when his gaze began to move across her face, Kate had the feeling he was searching for something, something that wasn't there.

And then he did the strangest thing. After giving his head a slight shake, he turned and walked away.

"Wait," Kate called after him.

When he paused, she moved quickly to catch up. "I'm sorry if I seemed rude. It's just that I forgot the agency was sending you over." She made a wry face. "I guess I was a little embarrassed to have been caught daydreaming."

She smiled. "If you'll come inside, we can have a cup of coffee . . . and I promise I'll be much more efficient during the interview."

Without waiting for an answer, she led the way to the backdoor. "I really am desperate for help," she said as she pulled open the screen. "My housekeeper is making my life miserable. Not that there's anything new in that, but she's been even worse than usual because we've been without help for several weeks. She's been using a couple of the neighborhood teenagers, and every day I have to listen to her complaining about the music they play while they work and how they never manage to get the job done the way she wants it done. So if we could work this out, you would be saving my life."

Kate didn't usually talk so much to a total stranger, but she was just a little unnerved by the way he continued to watch her. Silently, intently watching.

She poured two cups of coffee, took them to the table and nodded toward one of the chairs. "Please . . . sit down. As you probably figured out, I'm Kate Moore, and you're . . . ?"

He didn't answer immediately. Raising one hand, he wiped beads of perspiration from his brow and drew in several unsteady breaths.

A moment later, without meeting her eyes, he said, "Smith. McKinsey Smith."

He had the most unusual voice she had ever heard. Low, soft, and husky. A strange, almost erotic sound that shivered slowly down her spine and made the hair on the back of her neck stand on end.

She knew she was overreacting and told herself it was because this man had caught her in a vulnerable moment, the kind of moment Kate was careful never to let anyone witness.

Giving her head a small shake, she pulled out a chair opposite him and sat down. "Why don't you tell me a little about your past employers and what exactly you did—"

Before she could finish the question, the phone rang. Excusing herself, Kate rose to her feet and picked up the kitchen extension.

"Douglas!" she exclaimed with pleasure a moment later. "When did you get back?"

As she listened to the deep voice on the phone, Kate's attention kept straying to the man several feet away, who was still watching her closely, openly listening to her conversation.

"I'm glad you had a good trip. Did you . . . I'm sorry, I can't tonight. I'm having someone for dinner. Veda's first husband, as a matter of fact." She laughed. "It's an inside joke. Junior Thibideaux is coming for dinner, and no, you can't come too. You know you make Junior nervous. You do it on purpose, which, I might add, is very childish of you."

When McKinsey Smith shifted in his chair, she glanced again in his direction. His expression had changed. The stunned, nervous look had been replaced by something she couldn't interpret. Anger? Pain?

"Can you call me back later, Douglas? You've caught me right in the middle of something."

Hanging up, Kate turned back to the man at the table. "Is something wrong? Are you ill?"

With visible effort, his features relaxed and he shook his head. "I'm fine," he said.

Kate didn't press him, knowing that some men resented being ill and saw it as a sign of weakness.

When she regained her seat, she noticed curiosity in his eyes as he glanced at the piles of papers on the table. "I work here sometimes," she explained. "Even though Veda gives me hell for being in her kitchen."

"What kind of work?"

She took a sip of coffee. "Have you seen the Quick Care Car Centers?"

He frowned in concentration. "The red-and-white car washes? I must have passed a half dozen of them on my way here."

"Not quite. I have only six in the whole Dallas–Fort Worth area." She smiled when she saw his surprise. "Yes, they're mine. I started the first one four years ago. Now I have ten across the state and I'll be adding two more to the Houston area in a month or so. Next year I plan to—"

At that moment the back screen slammed with a loud bang.

"Okay," Ben said as he slid to a halt beside her. "Okay, I got it this time. I'm gonna put up the walls first, then I'll cut out the windows and a door. That way—"

He broke off and let his gaze drift over the man who was slowly rising to his feet.

The room was suddenly electric with some kind of energy, energy that seemed to come directly from McKinsey Smith.

The tendons in his neck stood out as he swallowed twice, his gaze never leaving Ben's face. He was openly staring at her son, just as he had stared at Kate earlier. But this time there was something different in his eyes. It was a poignant mixture that contained equal elements of urgency and joy and uncontrollable sadness, and she wondered if her son had somehow evoked painful memories for him.

"This is my son," Kate said quietly. "Ben, this is Mr. Smith. He's applying for the handyman job."

"How handy are you?" Ben asked, his gaze measuring. "Do you know how to build a treehouse?"

McKinsey Smith nodded.

"You're hired," the boy said, then turned to take an apple from a bowl on the counter.

"Ben!"

He glanced back at his mother. "I won't take up all his time. You can use him too."

Climbing the step stool, the boy sat on the counter and began rubbing the apple across his stomach to polish it. "The sink in the little bathroom sounds like this when the water drains out." He made a vulgar noise. "It makes me laugh, but my mom says some people won't think it's so funny. I guess she's talking about Mr. Allbright and Gardner Irwyn Bennett. They don't think anything is—"

"Enough!" Kate said, swallowing with difficulty to keep laughing. "We're trying to talk business and we don't need you here while we're doing it."

Ben jumped down from the counter and gave the stranger one last look of appraisal. "I think you'll do just fine. Your fingernails aren't shiny."

"And you figure the mark of a real man is unmanicured nails?" McKinsey asked in his husky-smooth voice as he raised one brow in inquiry.

"Right." Ben gave a short, succinct nod. "And we need a *real* man, don't we, Mom? Veda says—"

"*Get . . . out*," Kate said slowly and clearly. She had heard enough about real men for one day.

A moment later, with a flurry of movement and the slamming of a door, Ben was gone.

"I'm sorry for the interruption," she apologized. "I've never been able to convince Ben that I'm the adult and he's the child."

Once again taking her place at the table, she gestured for McKinsey Smith to do likewise.

"The work that needs to be done around here isn't complicated," she told him. "Simple repairs, some basic carpentry. I'm sure you could handle it." She glanced up, meeting his eyes. "Did you bring references? The people at the agency probably told you I was too fussy about who works for me, but the truth is, since whoever I hire will be living over the garage and will therefore have extensive contact with my son—whether they want to or not," she added wryly, "good references are essential."

"Ralph Seuter will give me a recommendation."

She blinked twice. "You know Ralph?"

Ralph Seuter was her late husband's best friend and mentor, the man who took David in after his grandmother's death. But Ralph had also been a friend to Kate as well. Without Ralph, she wasn't sure she could have survived after the death of her husband.

"Ralph sent me here," McKinsey Smith told her, "not the employment agency."

Smiling, Kate exhaled a sigh of relief. "You must be a saint if Ralph is recommending you. He's very protective of both me and my—"

"I'm back," Veda said, stating the obvious as she walked into the kitchen, her left arm weighed down by a canvas shopping bag.

Kate rolled her eyes. What she didn't need at

the moment was another interruption. "Veda, this is Mr. Smith," she said without bothering to hide the frustration in her voice. "He's here to apply for the job of caretaker, and I'm *trying* to interview him."

After putting the canvas bag on the counter, Kate's housekeeper turned to look at McKinsey Smith, who had risen to his feet at her entrance.

Veda slowly let her gaze drift over him. "What's that?" she said suddenly, pointing to a place behind him.

When he swung around to look, Veda took a moment to examine the posterior part of his anatomy, the part covered by tight-fitting jeans. Smiling in satisfaction, the older woman glanced at Kate and held up all ten fingers.

McKinsey Smith turned back around and glanced from Veda to Kate. "I didn't see anything."

"My eyes must be playing up on me again," the older woman said with a shrug. "Do you have a tool belt?"

He stared at her for a moment, then a slow smile twitched at his strong lips. "I can get one."

Both women simply stood and stared, both amazed and fascinated by the smile that had momentarily changed him into a different man.

"You do that," Veda said, flirting openly now. She shot a look in Kate's direction. "Hire him."

Amused and exasperated, Kate turned back to McKinsey Smith. "I'll check with Ralph, but it looks like you've got a job. I'll show you the apartment now, and we can discuss your salary. Can you start tomorrow?" She paused. "That is, if you want the job."

"I want it," he assured her. "But if it's all right with you, I'll get here early tomorrow and look at the apartment then. As to the salary, pay me whatever you think is fair. A safe place to sleep, regular meals, that's more than I've had in a long time. A long time," he repeated in his husky-whisper voice as he opened the backdoor and left without another word.

"Strange man," Kate muttered, staring at the door.

"Interesting face," Veda countered as she moved to the counter and began to unpack the groceries. "Personally I like that rugged, mountain-man look. Did you notice his eyes? Unusual."

"Not that unusual. David had eyes that color." Kate had noticed his smoky-gold eyes immediately. "The shape was different, but the color is the same."

"I'm not talking about the color. That man's history is in his eyes. You don't get that look from picking daisies. I'd say our new handyman's been on a couple of tours through hell."

FOUR

"You could at least have given me some warning," Ralph scolded. "When Kate called and started asking questions about McKinsey Smith, I almost didn't catch on in time."

David carried the portable phone across the room and stood next to the window that looked down on the backyard.

It was the evening of his first day at work. While Ben had been at school and his mother had been out attending to car-wash business, David had followed Veda around as she pointed out the things that needed doing in the house and yard, taking mental notes as she talked about Kate and Ben and life in general. During his lunch break, he had moved his few possessions into the apartment over the garage.

Six years ago the small apartment had been used

as guest quarters. A place, well removed from the house, for his wife's parents to stay during their frequent visits so that she wouldn't be shy about making love while they were there.

The apartment was more utilitarian now, the furniture and colors hotel-room neutral. An attempt, he guessed, to let each occupant add his own personality to the room.

David would add nothing. The three-room apartment was neat and clean and it had a strong lock on the door. That was all he needed.

"A handyman?" Ralph continued with disbelief. "What in hell were you thinking? Remember that lamp you made in shop? Damn thing nearly electrocuted me. I don't want to hurt your feelings, son, but the truth is you were always a dead loss with tools."

"Not anymore." David's lips curved in a wry smile. "You find out you can do a lot of things when your life depends on it. I've had six years worth of experience at manual labor."

Ralph swore quietly under his breath. "Where were you last night?" The older man was no longer trying to hide his anxiety. "When I found out you hadn't told her, and you didn't come back here, I got worried."

"I'm sorry. I spent the night driving around. I needed some time to think." He dipped his head and pushed a hand through his hair. "I couldn't tell her, Ralph. I almost did several times, but then I would start thinking about—" Breaking off, he shook his head. "I just couldn't."

"I was afraid the changes would hurt you," Ralph said quietly.

David drew in a slow breath. "I knew it would be different. I knew life wasn't going to stop just because I wasn't here to see it. But I thought I could deal with it. I was wrong," he admitted in his low whisper. "I found out I couldn't simply walk up and say, 'It's me. I look different, I sound different, but nevertheless it's me. Make room for me.'"

In the past six years David had spent a lot of time thinking about what he would do when he finally got back to Dallas, but he had never given a thought to the problems his resurrection would create.

"You didn't tell me she was the Car-Wash Queen. There's one of the damned things on every corner and she owns them." He paused, his fingers reflexively clenching the phone. "It looks like she's been having herself a high old time while I've been gone. How does she keep track of all the men?"

Kathy had been a virgin when she and David married. Totally trusting, totally giving. Sweet and shy in bed.

The woman who hired him wasn't shy.

Yesterday, after leaving the house, David had gone to the public library to look through back issues of local newspapers and magazines, making copies of every article that mentioned her name.

Later he parked on the side of the road and concentrated his attention on the years after his alleged death, discovering that the articles contained more about her personal life than about her business. It seemed that this *Kate* went through men like hand towels.

"That's not all there is to it," Ralph told him now, his voice gruff. "You didn't back out of telling her just because she's a successful businesswoman and, as a widow, has a few men friends."

Yesterday, when David had heard her talking on the phone to one of her men and realized that this man as well as others had been touching her, loving her, he wanted to lash out at her and them. He wanted to spread his pain around, let them all share in it.

But Ralph was right. That wasn't the real reason he hadn't told her who he was.

"I couldn't find Kathy in her," he said slowly, hoarsely. "I don't know this woman. She's beautiful. She's sexy as hell. But I don't know her."

His gentle, vulnerable Kathy was gone. Kate had taken her place.

David's need for his young wife had never gone away and never diminished. During the six years he had been held hostage, the only thing that kept him alive was his desperate need to get back to Kathy.

But just like in the dream, Kathy was gone. And once again David was left alone in the maze.

"No, not alone," he said suddenly.

"What?"

"I'm not sure about a lot of things, Ralph. I'm still trying to sort everything out in my mind, but one thing is absolute and unchanging. I have a son."

There had been something in one of the latest newspapers, in the society column, that David hadn't been able to get out of his mind. The columnist had hinted that marriage was imminent for Kate Moore, and it seemed that everyone in town was making bets on who she would choose to be her next husband.

"I took the job without really knowing what I was doing," David said slowly. "I think I simply wanted to hang loose for a while, look things over while I figured out what to do. But I'm glad I did. I need to get closer to Ben, see how his mother's plans for the future are going to affect him. I need to be with him, Ralph. I need to make sure my boy is healthy and happy. And that he stays that way."

"And if not?"

David shook his head. "I don't know. I'll think about that when the time comes."

Cutting the connection, he dropped the phone and moved to sit in a wide armchair near the window.

Ralph was frustrated. Frustrated and worried.

He needed to hear David's assurance that everything would be all right. He needed for David to open up to him. But there were things David couldn't talk about. Not yet. Not until he had worked them out in his own mind first.

For starters, he needed to find the reasons behind the anger and resentment he felt for the woman who used to be, but was no longer, the woman he married.

David's lips twisted in a wry smile. Adjusting to freedom wasn't as easy as he had thought it would be.

How much of his present disorientation was due to lack of sleep? he wondered. Would there ever come a time when he would be able to pass a whole night without waking in a cold sweat? When would he stop feeling nervous about going where he wanted to go and doing what he wanted to do? When did the word "free" start to have real meaning?

When the door opened, David glanced up sharply. He was on his feet in a defensive stance well before Ben stepped into the room.

"I knocked," the boy said by way of explanation, "but you didn't hear me. I knew you were in here 'cause I saw you when I was up in the cedar tree."

Letting out a slow breath, David regained his seat and forced his muscles to relax as he studied this boy who was his son.

Seven. His son was seven years old. He couldn't quite take that in. Last time David had seen him, Ben had been a chubby toddler. A baby. And now he was half-grown.

It took all of David's strength to keep from grabbing the boy and holding him in his arms. Dear God, he hated having to play the stranger to his own son.

But that would change, he assured himself. He simply had to be patient. Catching up on all the years he had missed would take time.

"I'm hiding," Ben told him now.

David raised one brow. "Is that right? You're not doing a very good job of it. I can still see you."

The boy giggled. "Not from you, silly. From Uncle Julian. He told me to call him uncle, but he's not, so I don't see why I have to call him that."

Ben moved as he talked, looking around the room, inspecting it. "Don't you have any pictures?" he asked, glancing over his shoulder. "I have pictures all over my house. Aunts and uncles . . . real uncles, not like Uncle Julian. Some cousins and one dead grandpa and one alive grandpa, and one almost one—that's Ralph. And there's lots of pictures of my dad."

He stopped walking and swung around. "Want to see a picture of my dad? I can sneak back in without them seeing me and get one to show you. I like the one where he's riding a horse best. He doesn't look like a cowboy, though. He looks more like one of the policemen who ride around in the park. But not exactly like that either. My mom says he was a teacher at a college and he taught 'nomics and that's about buying and selling stuff. He's dead now."

He said the last words flatly, as though he were talking about something he had seen in a movie, as though his father's death had nothing to do with reality.

David rose and moved to the window, his back to the boy. "Do you miss him?" he asked softly.

"Sure. He got dead when I was little, so I don't remember him, but I pretend like I do. I look at the pictures and pretend like I remember riding the horse with him or playing baseball, stuff like that. Sure I miss him."

When David turned around again, Ben gave him a hard look. "But that doesn't mean my mom has to marry one of her friends just to get me a dad. None of them would work anyway."

"Why not?"

Shaking his head, Ben rolled his eyes in an expressive gesture. "They're all geeks. Well, Junior's okay, but not . . . but not sporty. He just wears suits. You can't do sports in a suit," he said in a voice rich with contempt. "Everybody knows that. If I need a father like Veda says I do, I don't see why I can't pick out one I like. I could find somebody a zillion times better than Junior or Mr. Allbright or Uncle Julian."

David grinned. "Think so?"

"Sure. Like Mr. Sherwood, Bobby Sherwood's dad. His other wife left with a somabitchin' cowboy, so he doesn't have one right now and that's why I brought him home to show my mom. And he liked her just fine. He told me so. He wanted to take her to a place where they have contests to see who can drink the most beer and eat the most peppers without getting sick." He sighed. "But she didn't go."

David swallowed a laugh. "Mr. Sherwood sounds like good people to me. What did she have against him?"

"Girl stuff," he said, rolling his eyes again. "She said he says too many bad words and he spits. She talked to me and talked to me about how it's unfair to not like somebody just 'cause they're different from you, but she doesn't like Mr. Sherwood just 'cause he's different from her. She says it's not the same thing. She said she would defend his right to spit until she was dead. But she said she has some rights, too, and it's her right to choose friends who don't spit."

This time David couldn't hold back his laughter. Shaking his head, he said, "You sure know a lot of words for a seven-year-old."

Ben nodded. "I had my brain tested last year."

"Yeah? How did it come out?"

"They said I had a real good one. They wanted to move me to the third grade, but I didn't want to, so my mom told them no. I have private lessons where I can be smart, and at school I can be just as dumb as the other kids."

"That sounds like a good plan," David said, abruptly turning away again.

He had begun to pace before he realized what he was doing. Dammit, he was acting like a first-class jackass. He was getting all bent out of shape because this *Kate* had handled Ben's schooling the right way.

Drawing in a slow breath, he reluctantly admitted to himself that he didn't want to approve of anything she did. It would be much easier if he found only fault in her.

Making an effort to relax his tense shoulder muscles, he unclenched his fingers. He would have to watch that. If he was going to make the right decisions, decisions that would affect Ben's future, David had to find a way to be objective.

Kate walked out the backdoor and stood on the porch, glancing quickly around the yard. When she heard laughter coming through the open window of the garage apartment, she immediately headed in that direction.

At the top of the wooden stairs she found the door open. Although she could see her son clearly, McKinsey Smith was out of her range of vision.

Ben, seated in an armchair across the room, was bent over at the waist, roaring with laughter as he yelled, "Do it again, Mac, do it again!"

A moment later the boy straightened abruptly, his laughter fading. "Why are you putting your shirt back on? I want to see your muscles jump again."

And then Mac was standing in the open doorway, facing her as he used the tips of his fingers to tuck his dark shirt back into his jeans.

"Ben," he said, without taking his eyes off her, "you've been found."

Moving past him, Kate put her hands on her hips and looked down at her son. "I apologized to Julian for you and he was gracious enough to accept, but it better not happen again. I mean it, Ben. Next time you're rude to him, I'll let him read you another bedtime story."

"You wouldn't really," Ben said, staring at her in undisguised horror.

"Oh yes, I would."

"It'd be better if you starved me. Or locked me in the closet with a bunch of black window spiders. Or cut off some of my fingers." He glanced at Mac. "He reads baby books. Last time it was Rumblesticken . . . and he used *voices*." He rolled his eyes. "Like he's really going to sound like a princess. Yeah, right."

"Can it, short stuff," Kate said, struggling to keep her face straight. "Go back into the house, go into the living room, and tell Julian good night. Then go up the stairs, into the bathroom, run some water, and get into the tub. Understand? All the way in. And put on clean underwear this time."

Ben left muttering, "Well, I won't call him Uncle, because he's not my uncle and I don't see why . . ."

She glanced at Mac, smiling an apology. "I'd better warn you right now. He'll take over your life if you let him." She frowned. "Good grief, I forgot to tell him to use soap. He always manages to find a loophole. What is it about little boys and baths?"

As she turned to leave she added, "I'm sorry he bothered you. Feel free to tell him to get lost. I can't guarantee that it will work, but feel free to try."

"He wasn't bothering me."

Something in his voice, strength or determination, something that had been missing the day before, had her slowly turning back to him.

"He was hiding from your boyfriend," he continued. "And from what he told me, I'd have to say he acted with great prudence. 'Uncle Julian' sounds like the kind of man any sane person would hide from."

She blinked in confusion, and a moment later angry heat rose in her face. "What business is it of yours?" she asked tightly. "Just because my son invaded your privacy, that's no reason to invade mine in return. Is this how you normally speak to your employers? If it is, it's no wonder you were looking for a job."

When she finished, silence spread across the room, silence that apparently bothered her a lot more than it bothered McKinsey Smith.

"This didn't come up at the interview yesterday," he said finally, the words lazy and raspy soft, "so you can't really blame me for not following the rules. Am I supposed to prostrate myself when you walk by or simply pull my forelock? Maybe you prefer something more subtle. How about if I acknowledge by my self-effacing demeanor the difference in our social and financial status?"

Unbelievably, there was amusement in his husky voice and in his smoked-honey eyes. The idiot was laughing at her.

Who was this man? What was he? Every word he spoke showed that he was intelligent and educated. So why had he taken a job as her handyman?

She was going to have a long talk with Ralph, she decided with a frown.

"Don't be ridiculous," she said finally. "The only thing I expect from you, other than a job well done, is politeness. Plain, old-fashioned good manners. Surely—"

Breaking off, she blinked twice. When had he moved? McKinsey Smith was much closer than he had been before. Too close.

Keeping her breathing regular, Kate kept her chin up, resisting the urge to back away from him even when he moved a step closer. He might as well find out right now that she was not the kind of person who was intimidated easily.

And then, in an unbelievably outrageous move, his gaze dropped to her body and he focused on the low V of her blue silk blouse. He took no pains to hide what he was doing. His expression was openly insulting. And just as openly sexual.

To have turned away from his examination would have been a sign of weakness, so Kate simply stood there, unmoving, as he continued to stare, letting his gaze linger long enough for her to feel tongues of electric heat licking at the exposed flesh between her breasts.

With a soft laugh, he slowly lowered his gaze to the wide black belt at her waist, then to the black palazzo pants that fit smoothly across her hips.

And every place his gaze touched, Kate felt the heat.

A moment later, in a sudden flash of awareness, she realized what he was doing. McKinsey Smith was testing her. Goading her. He was looking for vulnerability, pushing her again and again in an attempt to discover her breaking point.

He wouldn't find it, she assured herself. Kate's vulnerable side was too well hidden. She had learned a long time ago to show the world a false face.

The crazy part was, it was no longer false. If you pretend often enough that you're strong, you become strong.

Even so, she decided it was time to put an end to the standoff. She had no time for games, subtle or otherwise.

"I'll get back to my guest now," she said, allowing her lips to curve in a polite smile.

"You do that." His voice was without inflection, but his eyes, those absurdly sensuous, incredibly knowing eyes, sparkled with laughter.

As though he had won.

Well, he hadn't, she told herself as she walked down the stairs. There was no question about it. Kate had won.

She stopped abruptly in the middle of the yard. Won what?

Heaven help her, she was going out of her mind. And it was all McKinsey Smith's fault. His little game had left her flushed and restless, making rational thought difficult.

She ought to fire him for that. She ought to go back right now and—

Kate couldn't fire him. Veda would kill her. And

what was worse, if she fired him, he would think she was doing it just to get back at him for winning. Which he definitely hadn't.

Laughing aloud, Kate began to walk toward the house.

Her new handyman might be the most confusing, most annoying, most arrogant employee she had ever dealt with in her life, but if she was totally honest, she would have to admit the encounter had left her feeling more exhilarated than she had in a long, long time.

FIVE

Holding her dress together at the back with one hand, Kate left the bathroom and walked back into the bedroom. The floor-length black satin gown made soft rustling sounds as she moved.

"If you had a crown and a stick thing with a diamond on the end, you'd look like a queen, but your dress should be white not black, 'cause you're not the evil queen. Evil queens never have blond hair. It's black. And their fingernails—"

"Stand on that chair and do up my zipper, please."

"—have to be long and red," Ben finished as he began to tug at the zipper. "Sometimes their fingernails are green, but that's just when they're turning people into lizards and big ugly birds. I have a idea—why don't you go with us? Veda's taking me to see the new Mutated Turtles movie and when we come home Mac's going to teach us how to play Las Vegas sweat. That's a game with cards."

"Mutated Turtles and Las Vegas sweat," she repeated slowly. "Sounds mighty tempting. Mighty tempting. But I'm afraid I've already promised to go to this party with Mr. Allbright."

Ben made a big production of hopping off the chair. "But you said it's not a party to have fun. It's for business. You should have fun sometimes."

Stooping to give him a hug, she said, "You're a sweetheart and I love you for thinking of me. I promise the next time I go out, it will be just for fun."

"Yeah, but that's the neat thing. You don't have to go out. Just stay home and hang around with me and Mac. You'll like it. You will. You'll really like it. And he doesn't even spit," he finished in triumph, as though by not spitting, his friend Mac had found the way to world peace.

In Ben's opinion, their new caretaker could do anything. Although the treehouse was already under way, Mac hadn't taken the project out of Ben's hands. Ben was always there, sawing when Mac sawed, hammering when Mac hammered. They were building it together, which meant Ben would feel a real sense of pride when the job was finished.

Veda often said that the way Ben had so quickly

and so thoroughly attached himself to McKinsey Smith was a nonverbal, subconscious demonstration of the boy's need for a father.

Kate said, just as often, that if Veda would spend less time watching 'Oprah' and more time minding her own business, they would all be better off. And furthermore, she told the older woman, for a boy who was so desperate for a father, it seemed to her that Ben was just a little bit too choosy. He hadn't attached himself to even one of Kate's men friends.

Veda's reply to that was usually short, crude, and loudly expressed.

McKinsey Smith had been with them two and a half weeks, and Kate could fault neither his diligence nor his competence. The shelves he had built for the pantry were sturdy and well finished. The sink in the downstairs powder room no longer made sick noises. He kept the yard neat and repaired things before she even knew they needed repairing.

Within a week of his moving into the apartment over the garage, he had begun to lose his gaunt look, a phenomenon Veda found immeasurably satisfying. The fact that Mac had the good sense to like her cooking made the older woman hold him in even higher esteem.

After their verbal skirmish on the first day, Kate and Mac had settled into a relatively normal employee-employer relationship. They rarely saw each other, and when they did, they spoke only about his work. But that didn't mean Kate wasn't always aware of his presence. Somehow McKinsey Smith had added his essence to the house. His energy, that strange electric force, seemed to linger in everything he touched.

Veda and Ben saw him more often. And with them, he was different. With Veda and Ben, Mac didn't act like an employee, nor did they treat him like one. They both looked to him for advice and companionship.

Sometimes, when Kate had worked too hard or hadn't slept well, she felt as though McKinsey Smith, with his husky voice and watching eyes, was trying to steal her family from her, a feeling she considered unworthy and did her best to ignore.

Putting her new employee out of her mind, she moved across her bedroom to stand in front of a full-length, wicker-framed mirror, checking her appearance one last time, making sure her dress was hanging the way it was supposed to hang and that not a single lock of hair had pulled free of the old-fashioned Psyche knot at the back of her neck.

"Okay," she told Ben, "I'm put together."

"Is he coming to get you?"

She shook her head. "No, I'm meeting him downtown. That way I can leave when I want to."

Ben nodded in understanding. "You mean when

he starts telling stories about when he lived in England and knew the minister."

Her son was a little too perceptive, she thought, hiding a smile as they left the bedroom together. Peter Allbright, a well-traveled, name-dropping stockbroker, could put a psychopathic killer to sleep when he started talking about the two years he spent in London.

They met Veda at the foot of the stairs. Tonight the older woman was dressed in freshly starched jeans, a sweatshirt that told the world it was encountering a "Wild Thang," and designer running shoes.

"Ready for a movie, champ?" Veda asked. "Well, come on then. Let's make tracks."

"In the mud?" came Ben's usual reply.

Kate laughed. "You two have a good time." She sent her son a warning look. "Do not, I repeat, *do not* put on your pitiful act and con Veda into buying one of those three-ton boxes of candy. Understand? You can have one bag of popcorn and one orange drink and that's all."

"Yes, ma'am." Leaning to the side, the boy looked behind her. "Bye, Mac. See you when we get back. Keep the cards hot for us."

Swinging around, Kate found Mac standing in the archway that led to the dining room. He must have followed Veda in from the back of the house.

He wasn't moving, his face showed no special

expression, but she could feel that peculiar energy of his spreading out across the room.

It was always like this. Whenever Kate was anywhere near him, she was suddenly filled with an unfamiliar restless excitement, as though she had just taken in a high dose of caffeine.

Pulling his gaze away from Kate, Mac smiled at the two people near the door. "The cards will be ready for action when you get back," he told Ben. "You two have fun."

When the door closed behind them, Kate sent an inquiring look in Mac's direction. "Should I lock up his piggy bank?"

He simply smiled, shaking his head as he turned to go back the way he had come.

Just then the phone rang, and as Kate picked it up she saw Mac pause and glance back, unabashedly eavesdropping on her conversation. Not that there was that much to hear, just her making understanding noises as Peter Allbright apologized profusely and at length for breaking their date at the last minute.

Moments later Kate replaced the phone and sent a wry glance in Mac's direction. "A minor crisis with his ex-wife," she explained. "Looks like the Moonlight Ball is out and a peanut-butter sandwich is in."

He didn't respond immediately. Leaning casually against the doorjamb, he concentrated on her face.

His smoky-gold eyes were calculating, as though he were trying to gauge her disappointment.

"I was just about to go out and get a bite," he said finally. "It won't be dinner at an exclusive restaurant followed by dancing in a ballroom full of the upper crust, but I think I can offer something better than sitting alone with a peanut-butter sandwich . . . if you'd like to come along."

Kate's eyes widened in surprise. During the two and a half weeks he had worked for her, Mac had made it clear that he resented her. She didn't know what she'd done to cause his resentment, but nonetheless it was there every time she encountered him.

Now, as she studied his face, she had the feeling this was something more than an offhand, spur-of-the-moment invitation. It was some kind of barely veiled challenge. A gauntlet thrown down.

"I guarantee where I'm going you won't run into any of your Junior League friends," he said when she hesitated. "No one will ever know you went to dinner with the janitor, if that's what's worrying you."

Her lips tightened and her chin came up. "That's not what's worrying me."

His eyes gleamed, his lips twitching with amusement. "Then what *is* worrying you?"

"Nothing. Absolutely nothing. It's just—" She broke off and drew in a slow breath. "Sure, why not? Give me a couple of minutes to change my clothes."

Upstairs, as she pulled on green slacks and a matching sweater, Kate held a silent argument with herself about the wisdom of accepting an invitation from a man who was a virtual stranger. A stranger who had done his best to irritate her almost from the moment they met.

It wasn't that she was afraid she would come to harm if she went with him. Something about the way he interacted with Ben and Veda had convinced her that he was totally trustworthy. And Ralph had recommended him. But he had a way of making Kate feel things she didn't want to feel. Too many things. Apprehensive and energized. Belligerent and vigilant and confused.

And then there was that peculiar restless excitement.

Not that it was necessarily a bad thing, she told herself as she brushed out her hair. Just different.

As she was slipping on her shoes, Kate realized, with considerable amazement, that she was looking forward to going out with McKinsey Smith.

Maybe she wanted to find out what it was about this man that so fascinated her son and housekeeper. Maybe she simply needed a break from the high-anxiety world of business. Whatever the reason, it had been a long time since she had really looked forward to a night out. A long, long time.

They took his car, an ancient blue Cadillac that seemed familiar, probably because she had seen several old cars like it in Ralph's enormous garage, and fifteen minutes after leaving the house, they pulled into the parking lot of a place that, according to the sign outside, was called Buddy's Shack, Home of Some Really Good Burgers.

Buddy's, a low, sprawling structure, had a stucco facade and looked like something left over from the fifties. Like all leftovers, it had been hanging around a long time, gathering wrinkles and losing charm, while someone tried to decide whether to keep it or throw it out.

"It's not as bad inside as it looks on the outside," Mac assured her, his smoky-gold eyes gleaming with amusement. "Besides, your patronage will probably put Buddy's on the map. As soon as Dallas finds out you were here, you won't be able to get in for the yuppies."

"Yeah, right," she said, mimicking her son.

He had lied. The inside was every bit as bad as the outside. Overscrubbed and underrepaired. Chipping linoleum floors. Little square tables with chrome-and-vinyl chairs. An enormous jukebox that filled the room with the nasal twang of country music.

On each table was a wide array of essentials. Salt-and-pepper shakers, napkin holders, and ashtrays. Sugar jars and little packets of artificial sweetener. Bottles, bottles, and more bottles, containing Tabasco, catsup, hot peppers, and steak sauce. There was barely enough room for food and none at all for elbows.

Buddy's had no waitresses. As soon as an order was ready, a dark, husky man enveloped in a white apron would yell, "Hey!" at which time everyone in the room would turn to see who the man would point to. The gesture meant that this particular individual's order was waiting to be picked up at the counter.

When it was Mac's turn to be yelled at and pointed to, he left the table and came back with a large brown paper bag. Written on the outside, in some kind of indecipherable shorthand, were the contents of the bag and, below that, the words "Green and sexy."

"What did you order that's green and sexy?" she asked, staring warily at the brown paper bag.

His laugh was a low, husky sound that drew the attention of the two women at the next table.

"Didn't you notice that Buddy didn't use a pad to take our order? He wrote it right on the sack. And then he adds something about what the customer is wearing so he'll know which order to give to whom." He smiled, letting his gaze drift over her green blouse. "Since I'm wearing a brown shirt, you were obviously the customer who caught his eye."

"Interesting system," she muttered, feeling heat rise in her face.

The hamburgers were, as the sign stated, really good. They were the old-fashioned kind, enormous and unwieldy, using freshly ground beef rather than flat frozen patties. The french fries were homemade as well, served up in big paper cups and dripping with grease. Dessert was fried apricot pies wrapped in waxed paper.

"Couldn't you find anything else fried on the menu?" she asked as she wiped a trail of juice from her chin. "There's enough cholesterol here to clog the state of Texas."

Mac shrugged. "If you're worried about the fat content, have another beer."

She glanced up and met his eyes. "Is this a new scientific breakthrough? Is there something in beer that counters the effects of too much fat in your diet?"

"No, your arteries will still be blocked, but after a couple of beers, who cares?" He paused, looking away from her as he crumpled his napkin into a ball. "There's something I've been wanting to ask you, but maybe it's not the kind of thing a hired hand asks the boss."

Kate took a sip of beer. He was, of course, referring to his first day on the job, when she had tackled him about his attitude. But tonight Kate was too mellow to be goaded.

"We're both off duty now." She moved her shoulders in a slight shrug. "Go ahead, ask away."

Setting down the long-necked bottle, he leaned back in his chair. As he studied her face he tilted his head to one side as though trying to figure something out.

"Why car washes, for heaven's sake?" he said finally. "Was it some secret childhood dream? Your one goal in life was to own a string of car-care centers?"

She gave a short, surprised laugh and shook her head. "No, it was nothing like that, I'm afraid. There simply came a time in my life when I needed something to do, something that would keep me active as well as make enough money to support me and Ben."

"I can understand that, but for someone with a liberal-arts degree, I would think—"

"How did you know about that?"

He began to shove their dinner debris into the paper bag. "I don't know." The words were low and husky, his tone casual. "Maybe Ralph mentioned something about it when he was filling me in on the job."

She smiled. That sounded like something Ralph would do. The older man was very proud of Kate and Ben and never hesitated to show it.

"I had some capital," she went on, "and the car wash—my first car-care center—was for sale when

I was ready to buy. It looked like something I could do, something that required no special knowledge. To expand, all I had to do was study the available equipment, figure out what worked best. Find people to install it and maintain it. Hire reliable workers to run the centers. I knew a little about marketing, so I spent some money on advertising." She leaned back and smiled. "That's all there was to it."

"I see," he said, nodding. "A little of this and a little of that, and you end up getting an award from the Chamber of Commerce and another from the Dallas Businesswomen's Association. No," he added when he saw her expression, "Ralph didn't tell me that too. I read about it in a magazine article."

"Checking up on me?" Her lips curved in a slow grin. "As a matter of fact, I did some checking of my own. I spent a good two hours pumping Ralph about you last week."

"And he told you about my six wives and fifteen kids?"

She shook her head. "For Ralph, he was amazingly discreet. He had already told me that you had worked for him years ago, but when I asked what you had been doing in the time between then and now, he got the strangest look on his face and said, 'Surviving.' That's all, just 'surviving.'" She drew in a slow breath. "I guess that's true of us all."

Later, as they were pulling out of the parking lot, Mac shot a glance in her direction. "Are you sorry you missed out on your fancy party?"

"You've got to be kidding." She gave a short laugh. "Let me tell you about the Moonlight Ball. Except for the gold foil crescents that are hanging from anything that will stand still, you couldn't tell this ball from any of the other 'important social events' that come along every year. Year after year after year."

She smiled. "From your crack earlier about the Junior League, I gather you've gotten the wrong idea about my social status. I don't run with that crowd."

"I seem to detect a definite lack of regret in your voice."

She laughed. "Yes, you're right. I like it the way it is."

"How is it?"

Kate considered the question for a moment then glanced at him. "You know how, when you throw a pebble in a pond, the circle at the center, the place where the pebble fell, is the strongest, the most well defined? Then as you go outward from the center, the circles get larger, but they lose force. That's the way society in Dallas works."

She settled back in the seat, her lips curving in a slight smile. "A set of concentric circles. There's a tight little knot in the middle. That's the Elite.

The best of the best. Males in this circle, while not necessarily the wealthiest, have all the power, and their wives pull all the strings. Just outside the main circle are the Worker Debs. All female. Their husbands have gobs of money, which allows them to believe that they're best buddies with the ones in the middle. In reality, they are the labor force. They organize and enlist and supervise. But, of course, their main function is to constantly reassure the Elite that they're still the center of the universe. After the Debs we have the Wannabee circle. They usually have just as much money as the Debs, but something is missing. They either don't have the background or the nerve to push into the Deb circle. When you hear about an enormous amount of money raised at a charity ball, it came from the Wannabee ring."

"Fascinating," he said, his voice dry. "Which ring are you in?"

"None of the above. My ring comes next. And technically speaking it's not really a ring. It's a faint little ripple that barely disrupts the surface of the pond. Those of us in this ripple are there simply because it's the only action in the pond. We go to these wonderful functions and drift around the outer edges, touching bases and swapping lies with all the other ripple dwellers."

She gave a soft laugh, then, intercepting his look of inquiry, explained, "Sometimes Ralph shows up, and he's like an oasis, a pool of reality in the middle of a politically correct desert. But that doesn't happen often enough. Most of the time it's deadly dull, and I go strictly to work the room."

"And it's important, professionally, for you to do that?"

She rubbed the tip of her nose with one finger, her brow creasing in thought. "I don't suppose it's absolutely essential, but it helps. If I didn't go to the parties and charity balls, I wouldn't get my name in the paper all the time, and that would mean missing out on a lot of free publicity. And then the Chamber of Commerce wouldn't know me from Li'l Abner. Those awards go to people who play the game."

"I take it that's a no."

She frowned. "I beg your pardon?"

"No, you're not sorry you didn't get to go to the ball," he said, reminding her of the question that had started her off on her tirade.

She laughed. "No, I'm not sorry. The truth is, rubbing shoulders with two or three hundred people is just not my kind of thing." Shooting a puzzled glance in his direction, she added, "What's that look for? Don't you believe me?"

"I was just trying to decide what your kind of thing is. Small, quiet parties maybe. The kind where you sit around on the floor, sharing good food and stimulating conversation with a few like-minded souls." He paused, smiling at her. "How am I doing?"

Too close. Much, much too close, she thought, looking away from him.

Mac had described the kind of parties she and David had once given on a regular basis. David loved entertaining, loved having interesting people around him.

Suddenly, in her mind's eye, Kate saw her late husband's face. That wonderful face. The comically questioning voice. The way he tilted his head to one side when he was trying to solve a puzzle.

The memories brought a surging wave of loneliness that made her voice sharper than she had intended. "You're not even close."

Sitting up straighter, she pushed the feeling away as she had done thousands of times in the past six years. "Now it's your turn," she said. "Was your one burning ambition in life to be a handyman for a bad-tempered boss?"

He smiled but kept his mouth shut and his eyes on the road ahead.

"Come on," she urged. "I told you about myself. You're a mystery man. Fill in a few of the blanks."

"Have you ever wondered what happened to D. B. Cooper?" he countered.

She laughed, recalling the famous skyjacking and the missing thief. "I won't be put off. You're intelligent and strong-willed—some might even go so far as to call you forceful. Those are leadership qualities. Why are you working for me?"

His continued silence brought Kate's stubborn streak out into the open. "Okay, I'll guess. You worked for Ralph when you were much younger, maybe to pay for your education. Then you went on to become a giant of industry, confidant and adviser to world leaders. After years of living only to make more money and gain more power, you reached a point where life became too complicated. Disillusioned, you decided to do a Thoreau. 'Simplify, simplify.' " She paused and looked at him. "How'd I do?"

"Right on the money," he said, nodding.

The amusement in his husky voice told her that she had missed the truth by a mile, but Kate was having fun now and decided to pursue his fictional life anyway.

"In the complicated part, there was of course a wife," she continued. "Maybe even more than one, because—"

She broke off when she felt the tension in the man beside her. This time she had struck a chord. His fingers had tightened on the steering wheel, his features harsh as he stared straight ahead.

"There was a wife," he acknowledged at last, his voice low and as stiff as his shoulders. "Only one, but as you said, it was complicated."

"Past tense. What happened?" She intercepted

the look he shot in her direction. "Yes, I know it's personal and none of my business, but you owe me one. On that first day, when I came looking for Ben, you as good as scolded me about one of my friends, and that's pretty personal, so that means I'm entitled. Or maybe not. But I'm still curious."

When the silence between them drew out, she wasn't sure he was going to answer, but then, with visible effort, he loosened his grip on the steering wheel and shrugged. "We changed. She changed. I changed. The two people who fell in love no longer existed."

"And the two people you became couldn't establish a new relationship?"

"When people grow, they don't always grow in the same direction."

She considered that for a moment, then said, "Children?"

The change in him was instantaneous and startling in intensity. Remnants of anger had been in his voice and face when she mentioned a wife. The anger was gone now, replaced by a confusing but potent mixture of emotions, reminding her of the way he had reacted when he first saw Ben. She had thought then that he must have lost a child. Now she was even more certain. Maybe that was why he had chosen to lose himself in a meaningless job. And maybe that was the complication that had caused both him and his ex-wife to change so drastically.

She had heard that losing a child was the most devastating thing that could happen to a marriage. Not many couples came through with their relationship intact. There was too much guilt. Too much unspoken and unshared pain.

For a moment, when Kate thought of how she would feel if anything happened to Ben, she felt an affinity for the man beside her, and she knew she would never again be jealous of his place in her son's affections. Ben had lots of love to give. If it helped Mac in any way, it could only be a good thing.

Later, when they reached the house and he followed her into the kitchen, she glanced at him as she opened the refrigerator door and pulled out a carton of milk.

"Are you sure you want to hang around and wait for them?" she asked. "It's still early . . . I mean if you wanted to go out again. Spending Saturday night teaching a seven-year-old how to play cards isn't exactly what you'd call an exciting evening."

"I want to," he said simply. "I like Ben."

"The feeling is mutual, but I guess you know that." She poured a glass of milk, then glanced at him. "Want some? I've gotten into the habit of drinking a glass before I go to bed. I'm pretty sure it doesn't do a thing to help me sleep, but at least I feel like I'm taking action."

He leaned against the counter beside her. "You have trouble sleeping?"

"Sometimes," she admitted reluctantly.

His gaze drifted over her face in a slow, careful study. "Everything, even a sleepless night, is a battle of wills with you."

She met his eyes. "Is that a statement or a question?"

"Let's make it a question."

"Then the answer is yes and no." Taking a sip of milk, she moved casually away from him. "There are a few areas in my life where I can relax. All the rest is a battle. That's not my choice. If you had ever been a woman on her own, trying to build a business as well as raise a son, you'd understand."

He raised one dark brow in inquiry. "What exactly does fighting insomnia have to do with being a woman in a man's world?"

She shrugged. "You get used to fighting. I have my safe places. Ben, Veda, Ralph. With them I can let down my guard and relax because I know there won't be any surprise attacks. The rest of the time—"

"You keep up your dukes," he finished for her.

"That's about it."

He was silent for a moment, still observing every move she made as though she were some kind of caged and labeled laboratory animal. "I notice you didn't mention Junior or Uncle Julian or any of your other friends as a place where you can let down your guard."

"No," she said quietly, "I didn't mention them."

Earlier, during dinner and the drive home, they seemed to have established some kind of rapport. There was almost a feeling of companionship between them. But now, as he pushed away from the counter and moved a step closer, the energy surrounding him was suddenly turned up to full power. It reached out to her and ionized the individual molecules in her body, making them sparkle and dance.

Giving him a wary look, Kate began to move toward the door. "I guess it's time for me—"

"I waited up one night last week," he said suddenly, "so I could see you when you came home from your dinner date."

What an extraordinary confession, she thought, turning back to him with a frown. "Why on earth would you want to do something like that?"

"I was curious."

Even though Kate was positive she wouldn't like the answer, she couldn't stop herself from asking the question. "Curious about what?"

"I saw what you looked like when you went out. I wanted to see how you looked when you came back." His gaze went to her shoulders, then to her breasts. "I was checking for fingerprints."

Instant, angry heat flooded her face. So much for companionship.

"You have no right," she said in a tight whisper, putting out of her mind the way she had questioned him earlier. "What I do with my life is *my* concern. No one else's. *Mine.*"

Although his lips stretched in a slow smile, his golden eyes glowed with the intensity that seemed to be an essential part of his personality.

"There's no need for you to get all hot under the collar," he told her. "Think of it as a quest for knowledge. I've noticed that you have a way of enticing a man, subtly but unmistakably beckoning him to come closer . . . and closer." He moved his shoulders in a casual shrug. "I just wondered exactly how close you let them come."

"That's none of your business," she said, her voice tight and hard.

"That's right, it's not. But that doesn't keep me from wondering. And since you said we were both off duty tonight, and since you decided to dig around in my personal life, I figured you couldn't hold it against me for wondering out loud, and maybe making a few casual observations."

There was nothing casual about him. And there never had been, she suddenly realized. When he had first mentioned having dinner together, she had sensed a challenge, one more move in their ongoing battle. Kate would have done well to keep that in mind.

The whole evening had been a sham. He had turned off the electricity just long enough to fool her into letting down her guard. And now that she had, he was moving in for the kill.

"Do you slap their hands when they reach for you, lady boss?" he said in the husky-soft whisper. "Is it another part of the game you play? Is it this secret battle of wills that's always going on with you? Veda says you choose men who don't demand anything of you. Is she right? Are they all a bunch of cold fish?"

"That's enough. I don't want—"

"It's easier for you that way, isn't it? You won't ever have to worry about your men being carried away by their sexual urges . . . because not one of them would know good, honest lust if it hit them in the face."

Her breasts were rising and falling rapidly, her teeth and hands clenched as she tried to regain her equilibrium. "I don't understand you. If I had come home, makeup gone, hair falling down, and a few pieces of underwear missing, that would somehow have made me a better person?"

She shoved the hair from her forehead in an angry gesture, her stance belligerent. "You say the men I date don't know about lust—well, there are obviously a few things you wouldn't recognize even if they hit *you* in the face. Things like personal integrity, fastidiousness, and good old-fashioned morals!" Kate was almost screaming now, equilibrium be damned. "How dare you try to make me feel inadequate just because—"

She broke off when she realized the man before her was laughing. He was *laughing*. At her. At her anger. At her righteous indignation.

As though he had stated it outright, she knew this had been his goal all along. He had deliberately set out to goad her into losing her cool. And she had fallen into his trap, as easy as you please and without looking back.

Damn his eyes.

Just at that moment Kate heard Ben and Veda come in the front door and made a conscious effort to gain control of her own emotions. Drawing in a deep breath, she willed her hands to stop shaking and forced her anger underground.

Before she left the room, she glanced at him one last time. "You think you're clever, don't you?"

"I get by," he said, his whiskey eyes still gleaming with amusement. "Yes, ma'am, I get by."

SIX

The dream began the same way it always did.

Kate was lying alone in bed, listening to the sounds an old house makes at night, when the door opened. In a slender stream of light from the hall she saw a dark shape, and a moment later David walked into the bedroom.

She turned her head to watch as he crossed the room and sat next to her on the side of the bed.

"I decided not to go," he told her. "If the great minds of the world want to talk to me, they can just come here to Dallas." There was a cocky gleam in his eyes as he slid down beside her and pulled her into his arms. "I'm not going to leave you and Ben, not even for a week."

"Oh David, I'm so glad." She rubbed her cheek against his shoulder, her heart leaping with joy. "I was trying to be strong. I really was. But I don't like being without you. I get so lonely."

"You don't have to be without me," he murmured against her lips. "Not ever again, Kathy."

"David—" She pulled her head back slightly, worry creasing her brow. "David, there was something I needed to tell you. Why can't I remember what it was? I'm sure it was important because it scared me so."

"Hush, baby. It's couldn't be that important. Nothing matters except that we're together now. Forever, remember?"

"Yes . . . yes, forever."

Holding her tighter, he moved to fit his body to hers. In the way of dreams, their clothes magically disappeared and she could feel his warmth easing its way into her flesh, comforting her, soothing away her fears.

It felt so good. This was how it always was with David. Their entwined bodies made a place that was safe and secure, separate from the worries and fears of the world.

When his hands began to explore her naked body, a long sweet sigh escaped her, and she moved shyly into his touch, telling him without words how much she loved him, how much she needed to have him here beside her always.

And that was when the dream changed. The

texture of the night fantasy was suddenly different. Unfamiliar.

There was an urgent excitement in the air as, with teasing, kneading hands, he began to do things he had never done before. This was no gentle easing into passion. He made no attempt to hide the rough, raw desire in his touch. Each move was bold and demanding.

She found herself shaken by sensations that were new and disturbingly intense. She couldn't catch her breath. Sighs became moans. Warmth turned into heat.

Arching her upper body, she pressed her bare breasts into the fevered touch, reveling in the pleasure aroused by the manipulating fingers. She was being driven by instincts so primitive and so powerful, thought became impossible. She could only feel.

"You like it, don't you?" The words were a rough, almost savage whisper that rasped across her ear. "Having my hands on you, touching you here and here, it's driving you right out of your mind, isn't it?"

Moaning again, she tried to comprehend what was happening. David had never asked those questions before. He had never sounded like that before. Something was wrong . . . no, not wrong, different. Crazy and wild and different.

She struggled to open her eyes, fighting to

raise lids that had grown leaden. When they were at last open, she blinked several times to clear her vision. Finally she could see. And what she saw made her pulse quicken and the breath catch sharply in her throat.

Even as she watched, the man in her arms was changing. His features were growing indistinct, blurred. Although she could still feel him, her fingers were still digging into hard, heated flesh, he was slipping out of focus, and soon only the eyes remained well-defined, the honey-brown eyes that had always fascinated her.

But, no, that was wrong. His eyes had changed as well. Something deep inside them had changed. They bored into her through the darkness. Powerful. Piercing.

There was no love, no tenderness in the look. Reckless passion was there, undisguised and uncontained. But mixed with the passion, somehow strengthening it, was hostility and open resentment.

And that was when Kate understood: The man beside her was not her husband.

With those passionate, bitter eyes, he watched her face, and knowledge of her discovery was there. And she knew without a doubt that her confusion gave him pleasure.

He slowly raised a hand and, still holding her gaze, began to touch her again.

She had to make him stop. If this man wasn't her husband, she had to get away from him. She had to leave him. Dear Lord, how could she lie beside him, shivering in anticipation, waiting for his fingers to reach her secret places, when he wasn't David? *He wasn't David.*

God help her, Kate didn't want to leave. It didn't matter that he was a stranger. It didn't matter that he was reveling in her emotional turmoil. Nothing mattered anymore except the fact that she needed this phantom's touch more than she had ever needed anything in her life.

Dear sweet heaven, he was—yes . . . yes, right there. Had she moaned aloud? *Please . . . please, again. Just a little more. Yes . . . yes!*

Her breathing was coming in harsh and rapid gasps, her eyes half-closed, the lids grown heavy with desire, and her avid gaze was drawn irresistibly to his hard, lean body.

She wanted to return his touch. She wanted to do to him what he was doing to her, make him feel what she was feeling. Her fingers curled with the overwhelming desire to feel the specter flesh beneath her fingers.

"Do it, Kate," came the deep-throated whisper. "You know you want to. There's nothing to stop you. Go ahead, take it. Take it all. All you have to do is reach out and—"

Kate woke up with the rasping, erotic whisper still lingering in the air around her.

Do it, Kate. Go ahead . . . take it all.

With a tiny moan, she reached up to brush the hair from her damp face. Her hand was trembling. Her body was trembling. If she could look inside, she would probably find that her soul was trembling as well.

Wide-awake now, she sat up in bed and wrapped her arms tightly around her knees.

It *was* David. It had to be. She had never dreamed of another man. She *wouldn't* dream of another man.

Drawing in a slow breath, she fought back the panic. She had to think this thing through calmly, using reason and logic. There was probably some obscure, psychological significance to the way her husband's features had become unrecognizable. A deep-seated fear of forgetting the man she loved. Or maybe it had been some kind of mental sleight of hand. Maybe she had imposed on David some of the changes that had taken place in herself.

But try as she might, she could find no explanation for the way her husband's voice had changed. Nor for the look in his eyes after the metamorphosis.

And that was when Kate, with great reluctance, allowed herself to acknowledge an idea she had been holding at bay since the moment she came awake.

The husky voice could have belonged to McKinsey Smith.

Groaning, she pressed her face to her knees, feeling the heat of embarrassment flood her body.

She couldn't be held responsible for her dreams. She had no power over them. They happened. They just *happened*.

Besides, she told herself, dreams never meant what you thought they meant anyway. Freud said that. Snakes were phallic symbols. Dying meant separation. Falling meant—

But Freud had also said that sometimes a cigar was just a cigar.

"I've been alone too long," she whispered in the darkness. Way, way too long.

Raising her head, she drew in another slow breath. So what if she had dreamed of McKinsey Smith? It wasn't anything to get in a panic about. She could, quite simply, have been attaching her suppressed desires to the last male she saw before the dream. If she had talked to her next-door neighbor tonight, she probably would have dreamed about him instead.

That made sense. Sort of.

Maybe not.

Try as she might, Kate couldn't imagine old Mr. Henson sending her into the kind of physical and emotional frenzy she had just experienced.

After David's death, Kate had gone in for grief counseling. She had passed through the predicted stages in more or less the predicted way.

But what she was feeling now, and what she had felt in her dream, hadn't been anywhere on the list.

They should rewrite the literature, she decided, moving a slow hand across her face as she leaned back against the headboard.

Someone should warn women that somewhere down the line, if they didn't remarry or take a lover, their bodies would go quietly and unexpectedly berserk.

David sat at the top of the stairs, his hands resting loosely on his knees. The apartment behind him was dark, the only light coming from a thin sliver of moon. He had been sitting in the same spot for over two hours.

As planned, David had stayed at the house to play cards with Ben and Veda. But not for long. Little more than half an hour had passed before Kate came into the kitchen to tell her son that it was time for bed.

She hadn't looked at David once. Not once.

Which told him she was probably still in a snit about the way he had baited her earlier in the evening.

Tilting his head back, he smiled, pleased by the thought. Maybe it wasn't exactly a worthy ambition, but from that first day when she had come to the apartment looking for Ben, David had recognized in himself a driving need to gain some control over the situation.

No, not over the situation, he corrected silently. Over her. He needed, in some small way, to control Kate.

For just a little while, when she was thrown off balance by him, when she was flushed with anger over something he had said or done, David was no longer a nonperson. When he challenged, when he pushed and prodded, when he managed to make her feel something, *anything*, David had substance.

Rising to his feet, he moved slowly down the stairs. Tonight he had asked her to join him for dinner with the intention of discovering more about her plans for the future, plans that would affect his son. But it hadn't worked out the way he had planned. She had fooled him. The tightly controlled Car-Wash Queen had loosened up and let down her guard.

It would have been much easier on David if he didn't have to acknowledge that she had feelings, that sometimes she was lonely, that sometimes she couldn't sleep.

He walked across the yard and into the shadows of the oak tree, grasping the swing rope with one hand as he stared at a knothole. A knothole filled with leaves.

David hadn't looked. Not once since he had been back had he cleared out the leaves to look inside. He didn't want to find out that squirrels had chewed the cork to bits years ago.

Moving to the other side of the tree, he leaned against it and stared up at her window. It was open, the top pushed down so that the air circulated through the room, stirring the curtains with each soft breeze.

Had she fixed up the bedroom the way she had dreamed of back then? He remembered the antique mantel she had seen at a salvage yard and fallen in love with on the spot. And a photograph, cut from the pages of a magazine, of a Colonial four-poster bed. Wallpaper samples of sage green and cream blended together in an uncomplicated design. Restful colors, she had told him, to ease away the tension left by any problems he might encounter at the university during the day.

His fingers tightened abruptly on the rope. It was Kathy who said those things. It was his sweet Kathy who dreamed those dreams. Kate probably preferred a Japanese futon to an old wooden bed. Lots of bold colors and sharp lines. Brutally minimalistic or whatever the in look happened to be at the moment.

Leaning his head back, he blinked twice and finally saw something he had been staring at for quite a while.

Kate stood in the bedroom window. She held the curtain back with one hand, her lower body pressed against the sill as she looked down onto the backyard.

For a while he simply stared at her, taking in her slender body and the sleek white gown that clung to each curve. Then, with steps that were slow and deliberate, he moved out of the shadows and into her line of sight.

He could tell the exact moment she spotted him. Her body went still and a moment later she stepped abruptly away from the window.

But then, just as abruptly, she appeared again, her shoulders straight, her chin high, as if to say, "This is my house and I'll look out my own window any time I damned well please."

"Still mad at me?" he called up to her.

"What?" She tilted her head to the side and frowned. "Oh, I see. No, I had forgotten how rude you were earlier. How nice of you to remind me."

He chuckled. "Why don't you come down and join me? There's something about a spring night that's very relaxing. Walking around in the shadows, feeling the fresh air, close up and personal, it helps."

"Helps what?"

He shrugged. "Whatever ails you. Indigestion. Insomnia. Sexual frustration. It's good for any of those."

"The way you concern yourself with my well-being is touching," she said with heavy sarcasm. "Really, really touching. But I think I'll just go back to bed."

He dropped his head back so that he could see her better. "Maybe you're right. If you came down, and we happened to talk, it would probably turn into an argument. Since it goes without saying that I would win, you'd end up all tight-lipped. Because it irritates the hell out of you when someone gets the better of you in an argument." Keeping his expression bland, David shook his head. "No . . . no, you're right. You should probably stay there . . . where it's nice and safe."

During his carefully calculated speech, her eyes had grown narrower, her chin coming up even higher. A moment after he stopped speaking, she swung around and left the window.

A low husky laugh caught in David's throat. She was coming down.

❧━━━━━━━❧

"That was so juvenile," Kate said as she closed the backdoor behind her. "I stopped calling people scaredy-cat to get them to do what I wanted years ago."

"Your loss." He moved his broad shoulders in a careless shrug. "As for me, I don't see any need to mess with a winning system. You're here, aren't you?"

When she laughed, he glanced at her. "I guess the milk didn't help."

"As a matter of fact, it did. I fell asleep right away. But—" She broke off and drew in a slow breath. "I had a dream."

"Must have been a doozy. Was it hot?"

Kate dipped her head, feeling the heat rise in her face again. Moving past him, she walked out into the moonlight that made silver streaks across the lawn.

"It was about my husband," she said over her shoulder.

"Do you dream about him a lot?" He had moved into the yard as well, but he stayed several steps behind, as though he were taking care not to crowd her.

"Not as often as I used to," she murmured.

"But something you said tonight brought back a lot of memories. Strong memories."

Frowning, she reached out to pluck a leaf from a flowering shrub. "This dream was different from the ones I usually have. It started out the same way. David came into the bedroom, just like always, and told me that he had decided not to attend the conference." She glanced back at him. "Ralph told you how my husband died?"

His face was hidden by the shadows of the cedar tree, and it was a moment before he nodded slowly. "He said he was taken hostage, then two years later he and seven others were killed in a mass execution."

Kate caught her breath. Why did it still feel like a knife in the heart to hear the words spoken aloud? She should be used to the truth by now. David was dead. Kate knew that, and yet something inside her—

"So in the dream he told you that he had decided not to go to Gamarra."

She blinked, suddenly recalling where she was. "Yes . . . yes, that's the way it always happens. He tells me that the conference isn't important and he's going to stay home with Ben and me. And then he—"

She broke off abruptly and cleared her throat. She couldn't believe she had almost told him the next part, the part where David started to make love to her, and how she always felt so safe, so loved, in those wonderful arms.

"But this dream was different," she continued slowly. "He was different. He looked at me as though . . . I don't know, as though he didn't like me very much. That's never happened before."

She could feel him watching her from the shadows. After a moment he said, "Maybe your guilty conscience is talking to you through your dreams."

The roughly spoken words make her draw back her head in surprise. "Why on earth should I feel guilty? I loved my husband. He knew I loved him. With all the unanswered questions, all the uncertainties surrounding his death, that's the only thing I am absolutely sure of. At the moment David died, he knew I loved him."

"Maybe," he said in his husky-whisper voice. "Maybe he did . . . at that moment."

There was something strange in the way he said the words, something strange about the electricity in the air between them, but before she could either comment or question, he stepped out of the shadows, and she saw that his expression was perfectly normal.

"You look softer in the moonlight," he said. "Softer and more vulnerable."

Her lips curved in a wry smile. "That should please you."

"Why do you say that?"

She moved her shoulders in a slight shrug. "I get the idea that you like shaking me up, that you take pleasure in trying to rattle me."

"Not only beautiful, perceptive as well," he said with a short laugh.

"Well, if you still have any doubts, let me assure you I'm human." She kept walking, feeling the cool grass beneath her thin slippers. "As human as they come, as a matter of fact. No one gave me a magic wand that I can wave around and have everything turn out right. I have to fight every minute to stay strong, to hold things together."

She threw down the mangled leaf and turned to face him. "I'm proud of what I've accomplished in the past four years. And I especially like knowing that I did it on my own, without having anyone standing by, waiting to catch me if I fall. But sometimes . . ."

She reached up to place a hand on her throat, suddenly feeling alone and without defenses. "Sometimes I get tired. Sometimes I get scared," she said, her voice low and soft. "When that happens I would give almost anything to have someone here to help carry the load."

She glanced at him and smiled. "It doesn't happen very often and luckily it doesn't last long. I get a good night's sleep and by the next morning I'm ready to go again."

"Superwoman."

The undisguised sarcasm in his voice brought a short sound of exasperation from her. "I don't know why I talk to you," she said. "You take every chance you get to provoke me. And here I am confiding in you." She shook her head. "It makes no sense. I must be even stranger than you are."

"You think I'm strange?"

"Definitely. Strange and scary. You always—" She broke off and frowned, examining his features in the moonlight. "There it is again. That pleased, satisfied look. You looked just like this earlier in the kitchen when you made me lose my temper. You loved it, didn't you? And now you're getting a big kick out of the fact that I find you a little frightening."

They had reached the oak tree by now. He leaned back against it, bending one knee so that his foot rested flat on the trunk.

"If you were scared because you thought I had a big, shiny ax hidden under my bed, that wouldn't please me," he told her. "But that's not the case, is it? What you find scary is the way I can get past the wall you've built." His lips stretched in a slow smile. "You don't like that. You don't like it one bit. You said it yourself—Ben, Veda, and Ralph are the only ones you let in. Everyone else stays outside the wall. Especially your men."

Kate wasn't even going to try to dispute his indictment of her. Every word he said was the truth.

"And you take that as a challenge," she said instead. "You see a wall, any wall, and you have to knock it down because it's the manly thing to do."

"Not any wall," he denied. "It's this particular wall that interests me."

"Why?"

A long pause followed her question. He stood staring through the darkness at her, his gaze holding her still, making her aware of the thin silk robe and even thinner silk gown she wore beneath it.

"Maybe I like the way your lower lip quivers when I unnerve you." He pushed away from the tree and moved a step closer. "Or maybe I'm being spurred on by instincts that are strictly humanitarian."

"Implying you would be doing a good deed."

They were fencing now, playing some kind of game that she didn't understand but couldn't back away from. Just like in the dream, she was held by a secret need of her own.

"Wouldn't I?" he asked. "If I took charge of a poor, frozen creature, warmed it up, got the blood moving in its veins again, wouldn't that be a good deed?"

Walking carefully around him, she took his place against the tree. " 'Poor, frozen creature,' " she repeated. "Not very flattering, and dead wrong besides. I'm not—"

"Yes, you are," he cut in. "You've lost your way, Kate. Somewhere along the way, you stopped developing. But it's even worse than that. You started to go backward. You forgot everything you ever learned about living and loving."

Although she hadn't seen him move, he was closer. He was slowly, gradually closing the distance between them. Her mind told her to keep up her end of the game. Parry. Pull back and revise her defense. But she might as well save her breath. The matter was out of her hands. She had to stay. She had to see it through.

"The crazy part is," he continued in a low voice, "it's so damned easy for me to get a reaction out of you. Why is that, Kate? Am I the only one who pushes the right buttons? Am I the only one who's curious about what would happen when your blood started to heat up and sensation returned to this beautiful body?"

She gave her head a short, awkward shake. "This is accomplishing nothing," she murmured. "If you'll excuse me, I'll go back inside now."

It was a poor attempt at bluffing and he recognized it as such. As though she hadn't spoken, he kept his gaze on her face, moving slowly closer un-

til his body was only inches from hers, close
enough for her to feel the heat, close enough for
her to feel his breath on her face.

"It was a little silly of you to think you
could hide from your own needs, wasn't it?"
he whispered. "Sexual desire is nothing to be
ashamed of. That's like feeling guilty for being
hungry when you have no food or thirsty when
you've gone too long without water."

His gaze moved from her face to her body
then back again, as though he were searching for
evidence that his words were bringing about some
visible change in her. Evidently he found what
he was looking for. His husky laugh whispered
across her face, and an instant later his hands
came up and settled on the tree on either side
of her head.

"It's been a long, dry spell, hasn't it, Kate?"

The space between their bodies was now too
small to notice, and when he turned just a little,
his chest grazed her breasts in a light, teasing
touch that shuddered its way through her sen-
sitized body.

"Who are you?" Her voice was hoarse with
shock. Shock and something else that she didn't want
to explore at the moment. Or maybe ever.

When he pulled back his head and blinked, the
sizzling, erotic energy dimmed for a moment.

"You know who I am," he said.

She shook her head once, then again, with more force. "No." She stopped and cleared her throat to make her voice steadier. "No, I don't. One minute I think we might grow to be good friends, and the next, you're doing something like this, something guaranteed to unsettle me. Every time we spend more than a few seconds together, you make it some kind of test. You turn on those wild, sexy vibes to get me all agitated. Or you come out with rude, intimate pronouncements designed specifically to make me lose my temper. It's like I'm a lump of bread dough that you poke occasionally, just to see if there are any changes in the consistency. And you still haven't told me why. If you acted the same way with Veda, I could say it was just something in your personality, but it's only for me."

"Only for you." He moved again, brushing his chest across hers, making sure she felt the rough caress on the taut tips of her breasts.

Kate closed her eyes and tried to draw back, tried to force the tree to absorb her. "What do you think you're doing?" she rasped out.

"I know exactly what I'm doing, but it's nothing for you to worry about," he whispered. "I'm just chipping away at the wall a little."

"Well . . . well, don't do it," she gasped.

"You don't have to stay," he told her. "You

can move away anytime you like. I haven't laid a finger on you."

He was right. Just like in the dream, she knew she could move if she wanted to. And just like in the dream, she knew she was going to stay.

A look of savage satisfaction settled on his features and he dipped his head so that his mouth was a warm breath away from her ear. "It's pretty pitiful, Katie, the way you lie in bed alone, having hot dreams."

Bending his knee, he slowly brought his left leg up between her thighs, gently forcing her body to accommodate the sensual intrusion.

"Just don't make the mistake of thinking those dreams are anything like the real thing. Do you want me to tell you what the real thing feels like?"

When she gave her head a frantic shake, he responded with a soft laugh. "No? Too bad, I'm going to tell you anyway. In real life, when you're lying naked in a man's arms, it's not a solitary sensation. You feel it in a dozen different places. The heat. The hardness. The slick, wet—"

"Don't—"

The protest died in her throat. This was too much. it went way beyond what she had felt in her dream. The teasing, tormenting stroke of his muscular leg between her thighs, denim through silk. The rough texture of his shirt grazing her breasts again and again. The warmth of his breath on her ear. It was all explosively erotic. And it was all real.

Even though the effort was becoming painful, she kept her body still. If he would just stop, she could reclaim her strength, she could find a way to fight what she was feeling. But he didn't stop.

"When he kisses your throat and breasts and stomach, you can dig your fingers into something real. You don't have to lie there and take. You can move, Kate. You can give. And at the end, when you come, all those beautiful spasms of pleasure aren't thrown out into empty space. They happen against a wet mouth or clasping fingers or hot—"

"No."

He ignored the harsh denial. Moving his chest, he let the hard, cold buttons on his shirt scrape roughly across the tips of her breasts. His leg was still moving between her thighs, up and down, again and again.

She was going into sensory overload. If she didn't do something, if she didn't make it stop, she was going to disappear in one violent burst of sensation. She had to move away. She had to force her drugged body to—

"You give everything that's in you at that

moment, Kate," he rasped in a slow, rough drawl. "And all that's left is peace. It's the best damned cure for insomnia that's ever been invented."

Through a red haze of pleasure, Kate realized her lower body had begun to thrust forward to meet each sliding stroke, again and yet again as she struggled to get more and more of the feeling.

With an inaudible cry of protest, she brought her hands up to his chest and pushed him away.

It took no effort at all. One little shove and she was free.

In her haste to get away from him, she stepped awkwardly to the side and stumbled. When he automatically reached out to help her, she drew away, ignoring his hand. She couldn't let him touch her. If he touched her again, she was lost. She wouldn't be able to leave him. She wouldn't ever be able to leave.

Regaining her balance, Kate moved quickly toward the backdoor and the safety of the house.

David watched the door close behind her, his fists clenched, his breathing harsh and fast.

After several long, tense moments he turned and leaned back against the tree. Only when he brushed a hand across his face did he realize that the tips of his fingers were raw from digging into the tree. It had taken every ounce of strength he possessed to keep them on the rough trunk, to keep them off her body.

Drawing in a deep, rough breath of air, he searched for calm. He pulled up survival techniques he had used against his enemies and forced his pulse rate to return to normal, forced his muscles to relax.

What in hell had he been thinking? He had wanted to leave her agitated and confused. He wanted, if only for a brief moment, to be an important force in her life.

Good God in heaven, he had been crazy to try something like that. Out of his freaking mind.

There was a riot inside him, but it was different from the panic attacks. David felt no urge to run and keep running. This particular riot was caused by an overpowering need to follow her into the house, go up to the bedroom, and finish what had begun here in the moonlight.

In the kitchen, Kate leaned back against the door, her knees weak, her breasts heaving, her breath coming in rough, urgent gasps.

She still couldn't believe what had just happened. All her defenses, defenses it had taken her years to build, were gone. And he hadn't laid a finger on her.

A semihysterical laugh caught in her throat. Never in a million years had she thought she could feel like this. She had read about it, she had seen it in movies, but this wasn't the kind of thing ordinary women felt.

With David . . . When her husband made love to her, it had always been gentle. Filled with laughter and love. With David, sex had always been fun.

"That wasn't fun," she said in a hoarse whisper.

It was more like being on a rowboat in the middle of a hurricane. A life-and-death thing.

And maybe that was what bothered her the most. An annoyingly attractive man had teased her in the moonlight, but to Kate, it had somehow felt *important*.

SEVEN

Reaching up, David yanked the cord dangling from the ceiling and the light bulb responded by sending down a yellow cone of light that illuminated the area immediately around him yet left deep shadows in the rest of the cavernous room.

The basement was large, measuring the length and width of the house and filled with the usual clutter found in such places. Boxes, tools, and one long wooden bench that substituted for a worktable.

Staying in the circle of light, he moved around and read the labels on the boxes in the immediate area. Some fell into mysterious categories. *Green K&K. FFQ. BBC/18 Mo*. Others were more easily deciphered. *Outdoor Xmas Lights. Grandmama's Blue China*.

And then there were boxes marked simply: *David*.

He opened several of them and spent a while sorting the contents. Books. Clothes. Fishing equipment. A collection of antique banks. Things that used to belong to him, back when he was alive and this was his home too.

When beads of cold sweat broke out on his forehead, David clenched his fingers into tight fists, sucking in deep, unsteady breaths to fight the rising panic, and eventually it began to ease.

There were still times when he would wake from a nightmare and spend the rest of the night pacing the floor, resisting sleep, refusing to be pulled back into the dark echoes of those six years. But the anxiety attacks didn't happen nearly as often now, and they didn't take nearly as long to fight off when they did.

His lips twisted in a tight, humorless smile. He knew perfectly well why the attacks were diminishing in strength. The truth was, the present was gaining power over him, and in the process, the past was being eclipsed. Since the night he had goaded Kate into leaving the sterile safety of her bedroom, memories of what happened under the oak tree overshadowed all other memories.

That night, after she left him, David had spent a few hours driving aimlessly around the city of Dallas, ignoring the lights and late-night action, held in the grip of lingering desire. He didn't come back until he was certain he could resist the urge to go into the house and up to the bedroom they had once shared.

David still wanted to do that. He still wanted to seek her out and finish what had begun that night.

Over and over again, he had relived those moments in the backyard. The way she looked when the breeze stirred her pale hair. The way those thin layers of white silk, insubstantial as a passing thought, clung to her hips and thighs, outlining and emphasizing her breasts.

Now, when the memory again brought an automatic tightening in his groin, he swung around and pushed fingers through his hair.

This is ridiculous, he told himself as he paced the area in front of the workbench. He was making too much out of the whole thing. So he had the hots for a beautiful woman. Big, freaking deal. It was a perfectly natural reaction. After six years of celibacy, being close to a woman like Kate would drive any man crazy.

He gave a short laugh. After six years Eleanor Roosevelt would have looked pretty damn appealing.

If he had any sense at all, he would go out, this very night, and find a willing woman, a woman who didn't come with complications, a woman who didn't drive him crazy. They were out there.

Hundreds and hundreds of beautiful women. All he had to do—

David abruptly cut off the thought. He was fooling himself. Lying through his teeth. He wanted Kate. No other woman, no matter how beautiful, no matter how willing, would do. He wanted *Kate*.

And in acknowledging that fact, David also had to acknowledge another one: His desire for Kate felt like a betrayal. Wanting Kate was somehow a denial of what he felt for Kathy.

Crazy.

"Hi, Mac."

Jerking his head around, David watched as Ben stepped into the small circle of light.

"Whatcha doin' down here?"

"Thinking." David unclenched his fingers and drew in a slow breath. "Just thinking. And what brings you to the nether regions?"

"Hiding. Just hiding." Picking up a screwdriver from the bench, the boy stared at it for a moment. "How about we pretend like this is a Mutated Turtle Super Swamp Saber?" He swished the screwdriver through the air. "That way we can zap the bad guys and turn 'em into sewer sludge."

"Who are you hiding from this time?"

The boy made a face. "Him," he explained, using the screwdriver to point toward the ceiling.

David glanced upward, then back to his son. "God? You must really have been bad."

Ben laughed, and when Ben laughed, he threw

his whole body into it. David laughed with him. He loved watching his son, loved the way the small brown eyes came alive with dancing gleams of light.

"Not God, silly." He drifted into the darkness, moving with sure steps through a maze of boxes. "Gardner Irwyn Bennett," he called back as he climbed over an old chest. "Every time, he brings flowers. And every time, he says this joke about how they're from Gardner's garden. Do you think he forgets he already said that joke? It wasn't even funny the first time. But my mom always laughs." Dropping to his stomach, Ben reached under a small table. "Not a real laugh, though. The kind of laugh like you're reading the words in a book. Ha, ha, ha. Like that."

"You're a pretty smart kid, aren't you?"

"I told you, they tested—"

"Yes, I know. They tested your brain and you've got a good one."

Frowning, David reached up to rub his jaw. Why in hell did she choose men whom his son had to hide from? Either she didn't know how Ben felt, or she didn't care.

She cared. There was no doubt about that. David had seen the way she was with Ben. Over and over again he had seen evidence that she was a good mother to his son.

Did she simply have a blind spot where her men were concerned?

When Ben returned to the circle of light, he had a plastic bag half-full of suckers clutched in one hand. "They're left over from Halloween," he explained to David.

"That was over six months ago."

"Suckers don't get rotten. I already ate all the good ones, though. There's only green and purple now." He held up the bag. "Want one?"

When David declined, Ben hopped up on the bench and began to swing his short legs back and forth. "See if my tongue is green," he said, poking out his tongue.

"That's disgusting."

The boy grinned. "Mary Katherine Prescott gave me some candy that makes your teeth and tongue glow in the dark, but my mom wouldn't let me eat it."

"That's tough." He sat down on the bench beside his son and spent a moment studying the miniature face. "Remember the day you came to the apartment and told me that none of your mother's friends would make a good dad for you? You were hiding from Julian that day. Now you're hiding again. Want to tell me what you've got against Gardner Irwyn Bennett?"

Ben shrugged, concentrating all his attention on the sucker. "He just doesn't want me around."

"What makes you think that?"

He shrugged again. "I guess 'cause he told me."

He glanced up at David. "It was the first time he came here, right before Christmas, and he brought me a present. It was a dumb present, but I told him I liked it anyway 'cause my mom was right there and she already told me to be nice. He kept saying I was a fine boy, but he called me Benjy, like he didn't even know that was a dog's name."

He talked in a constant stream, his swinging legs keeping time with the words. "Then my mom went to talk to Veda in the kitchen and Gardner's forehead made lines across it like cartoon sea gulls and he told me to stop bumping into furniture and don't touch the tablecloth 'cause my hands were dirty, and Jesus, can't I settle down. I told him he shouldn't say Jesus in a bad way, specially at Christmastime 'cause that's His birthday. And that's when he said don't talk to him 'cause kids give him nerves."

Ben paused to draw in a deep breath. "So I guess he'd like it better and I'd like it better if I just wasn't there. And that's why I came down here. See?"

David frowned. Ben didn't exactly sound traumatized. He was matter-of-fact about the whole thing, as though it were the normal course of events. But David didn't like it. He didn't like it at all.

"Why haven't you told your mother how you feel about him?"

" 'Cause it would hurt her feelings," Ben explained patiently. "She likes him, and she likes me, and she wants us to like each other. But he doesn't like me. And I don't like him. And I don't like how he acts like this is really his house, going around touching stuff that doesn't even belong to him. I want to tell him to settle down, but I wouldn't say Jesus with it 'cause—"

"What stuff?" David interrupted.

"Everything. Just everything. He picks up my dad's pictures and looks at them mean. Then he goes all around the living room, moving stuff on the shelves and tables like he's checking for dirt."

Ben's upper body rose and fell as he exhaled a loud sigh. "Gardner gives me nerves."

"I think he gives me nerves too," David muttered through clenched teeth.

For a long time David simply sat and stared at the wall. Then, rising abruptly to his feet, he glanced down at his son. "Want me to show you a secret?"

Ben jumped off the bench, looking intrigued. "Sure."

Picking up a folding ladder, he told the boy to bring along his Super Swamp Saber, and the two of them walked through the shadows to the opposite side of the room.

Five minutes later David was sitting at the top of the ladder and Ben was two steps below. On the wall, up close to the ceiling, was a small vent covered by a metal plate.

Years ago, when David discovered the vent's peculiar properties, he hadn't told Kathy. The next time she went down to the basement, he had called her name in a ghostly voice; scaring her to death. Although she had known David was responsible, she had never figured out exactly how he did it.

Putting a finger to his lips to warn Ben, David carefully removed the metal plate. Instantly voices came from the vent, as clear and sharp as they would have been had the speakers been in the same room.

" . . . know you don't like hearing this, Kate, but the boy needs a reliable masculine influence in his life."

David stiffened, automatically resenting the man's patronizing tone. Evidently Kate didn't care much for it either. When she responded, there was a definite touch of sharpness in her voice.

" 'The boy' is happy, healthy, and well adjusted. Why should I mess around with that?"

"There's no doubt that he's a fine boy. A *fine* boy. But you have no way of knowing what problems are brewing for the future. In a few years he'll be an adolescent, and that's a rough time, even for children with two parents. You have to prepare for that now. Face it, Kate, there's only so much you can do. The boy needs a father."

"Why do people keep telling me that?"

"You know that old saw. If three people tell you you're sick, lie down."

"I don't know . . . I don't know," she muttered, sounding harassed, exasperated.

A moment later, when he heard her apologizing to her guest, explaining that she needed to make a business call, David motioned for Ben to precede him down the ladder.

"They can't hear us over here," he told Ben when they reached the other side of the room.

"That was *so* awesome." Ben's eyes were wide with wonder. "How did you know it was there?"

"A lot of old houses do the same thing. But it's our secret, okay?" David paused, watching his son's face for a moment. "You were right about Bennett. He's a stupid twit."

Ben nodded and leaned over to scratch his knee. After a moment, without looking up, he said, "This kid I know, Jonathan Phillip Vintner, he used to live across the street. Not right across. Two houses down that way"—he used one finger to point over his shoulder in a general easterly direction—"and then across the street. He moved to El Paso, so he doesn't live there anymore."

David waited. There was something in the boy's voice, something in the way he avoided David's eyes, that told him this was more than a casual conversation.

"One time," Ben continued, "when we were

playing lost in the desert, Jonathan said sometimes R. J. hits him. R. J. is his stepdad. Only it wasn't spanking. Jonathan said R. J. hit him with his hand in a fist."

He stopped scratching his knee and began scratching his elbow, still keeping his gaze down. "Jonathan told his mom and she got mad and said he was just telling lies and she was going to send him to live with his grandpa in N'Arlins, Louisiana, and Jonathan thought that was okay because his grandpa didn't ever hit. But it hurt his feelings because his mom thought he was lying."

"That's too bad," David said softly.

Ben nodded. "Sometimes I think about Jonathan. Sometimes— See, he didn't go to N'Arlins with his grandpa. They took him to El Paso."

"And you wonder if R. J. is still hitting him?"

When Ben nodded, David sat down and pulled his son onto his lap. He was afraid for a moment that Ben would think sitting on laps was a baby thing to do, but the boy didn't protest. He scooted closer until his shoulder was pressed against David's chest.

Swallowing past the lump in his throat, David exhaled a slow breath. "Things like that happen sometimes, Ben. I wish they didn't, but they do."

Glancing down, he found that Ben was watching him closely. "It's not going to happen to you," he said, the words slow and precise. "Understand?

You have too many people watching out for you. Your mother, Veda, Ralph. And me. We wouldn't let something like that happen to you."

Raising his hand, he brushed the hair off the small forehead. "I don't think you should spend any more time worrying about Bennett. Just because he comes to visit your mother and brings her flowers doesn't mean she's going to marry him. Your mom's a pretty smart lady. She wouldn't get hooked up with someone who's a fake."

Ben turned his head away, but not before David had seen the apprehension in his eyes. "But what if she does?" Ben whispered. "What if he fools her? Even if he didn't hit me, he can't be my dad, Mac. He *can't*."

"That's enough," he said, his voice firm. "It's not going to happen."

Ben scratched his nose and muttered, "It might."

"It won't."

"It might."

"It *won't*. Because I won't let it. I won't— Are any of your mom's friends the kind of man you'd want for a father?" David asked abruptly.

Ben shook his head slowly. "Junior is nice, and sometimes Julian makes me laugh, but they're not *dads*. You know? They're just men."

David knew what Ben meant. None of them was genuinely interested in the boy. They were nice to Ben simply to get closer to Kate.

"So how many men are we talking about?" David asked.

"Junior and Julian"—he held up a finger for each man—"and Mr. Allbright and Gardner Irwyn Bennett. Russell married that tall lady with the pointy chin and she doesn't like my mom, so he doesn't come here anymore."

"What about Douglas?" he asked, remembering the call Kate received the day she hired him.

"Oh yeah, I forgot. Douglas has two houses. One in Dallas and one somewhere else. I think it's in one of the M states. So he's not here too much."

"Okay, that's five." David smiled. "Piece of cake. If you don't want them hanging around, we'll just have to get rid of them."

"Are we gonna shoot 'em?" Ben jumped to his feet, his eyes round with awe and what looked suspiciously like gleeful anticipation. "Wait, I got a idea. How about if we bury them down here under the floor? Nobody would probably ever find them down here."

David laughed and shook his head. "Bloodthirsty little monster, aren't you? I don't think we need to do anything quite that drastic. The two of us will just have to convince them that hanging around your mother is not what they wanted to do after all."

He went down on his knees so that he and his

son were eye to eye. "So what do you think? Do we have a deal?"

After wiping his hand on his shorts, Ben extended it to David. "Deal," he said earnestly.

David shook the grubby little hand and laughed in delight. "Okay, then. It's settled. Today we get rid of Suitor Number One." He paused. "You say Gardner Irwyn Bennett doesn't like kids?"

Ben nodded. "They give him nerves."

David's lips curved in a wicked smile. "Excellent."

Ten minutes later, when Ben left the basement, there was a purple sucker in his mouth and purpose gleaming in his small brown eyes.

Moving back across the room, David sat on the ladder and waited. Soon he heard the scuffling of his son's shoes on the wooden living-room floor.

"Where's Mom?"

"She had to make a business call." Bennett's voice was distracted, his thoughts clearly elsewhere. A moment later, however, that changed.

"Can't you be still? Why are you hopping? Hopping is for outside. When you're inside the house, you can't hop."

"Sure I can. It's easy. Watch."

"I didn't mean— Will you *stop that*?"

"Okay, but my muscles get jerky when I be still," Ben warned. "If you want, I can sit down by you and talk. Want to talk, Gardner?"

"As a matter of fact, I do."

In the moment of silence that followed, David pictured Ben settling down on the couch beside his unsuspecting victim.

"You like me, don't you, Benjy?" Bennett was calmer now, his voice smooth and friendly.

"Sure I do. I like you just fine."

"I'd like it if you told your mother that. And maybe . . . Why don't you tell her that you'd like for her to get married again? You would like it, wouldn't you, Benjy? Having a man around the house all the time, someone who could teach you how to behave and . . . and do activities with you."

"What kind of 'tivities?"

"I don't know." The smoothness was slipping just a bit. "Whatever boys your age do."

"You mean like playing dump trucks? Yeah, I like trucks. Are you going to marry my mom, Gardner?"

"I'd like to. And I would also like to be your father, Benjy."

"Cool. But I don't have to talk to her about getting married. See, we talked about that already, and she promised, cross her heart, that soon's she gets married, she'll have some more kids. That's on account of she was the only child and she didn't like it, so she wants me to have lots of brothers and sisters and that way I won't get lonely. We think five would be good. Do you want—"

"What are you talking about?"

"I'm talking about having kids." He paused. "But maybe you better marry her pretty quick, Gardner. It takes plenty of time to have five kids and she might get too old. Unless she had twins. My friend Casey Riggs, his mom had—"

"Kate never said anything to me about— What happened to your lollipop?" Bennett's voice was low and wary. "Benjy, didn't you have a lollipop in your mouth when you came into the room? Where did it go?" Wariness had now blossomed into panic. *"Where is it?"*

"Maybe I dropped it. Purple's not my best color. I like the yellow ones better but— Oh, there it is."

"Where?"

"Right there on the back of your sleeve. Be still. I can't reach it when you're wiggling. Now I got it. It has some fuzz on it, but that's okay. You can wash suckers."

"You malignant little son of a— This jacket is *cashmere*. Dammit, boy, you've smeared that filthy purple mess all over the back of the sleeve!"

"You might ought to get used to it, Gardner," Ben said sagely. "With six kids, somebody will probably always be gettin' stuff on you."

"I would slit my throat first," the man muttered under his breath. "Tell your mother . . . tell her that something came up and I couldn't stay."

The last words were faint. Exit lines, said on the way out.

David leaned back against the wall and laughed.

One down and four to go.

Kate walked into the living room, frowning as she glanced around. "Where's Gardner?" she asked Ben.

"He left. He said I was supposed to tell you that something came up. I like that dress. It looks like a tea party."

"That's all he said, that something came up? I was using the phone, so how could—" She sat down on the couch with a sigh. "Tell me exactly what happened, Ben."

Her son tilted his head to the side and squinted, a pose he always assumed when he had to do some heavy thinking. "We were just talking . . . um, let's see, I was telling him about how Casey got twin baby sisters and then . . . and then . . . oh yeah, that's when Gardner found a dirty place on his coat and his face turned red like he was holding his breath." He straightened his head, opened his eyes wide, and shrugged. "And then he said he had to leave."

Kate shook her head, a wry smile twisting her lips. Gardner was a good friend, but sometimes he could be a real pain. The care he took with his appearance bordered on the obsessive. He would have been mortified to find that anything about him was less than perfect.

"Do you think Gardner had bad manners from not staying to tell you about his coat being dirty?" Ben asked, breaking into her thoughts.

"Maybe." Shrugging, she rose to her feet. "Oh well, I guess I'd better go tell Veda to save the fancy stuff for another time."

Ben did a little hop-skip dance. "Yea! And we can eat in the kitchen with Veda and Mac and you can take your hair down 'cause when it's rolled up that's for business and tonight's just for fun."

"All of that," she agreed, laughing as she walked out of the living room.

She was halfway down the hall when the door to the basement opened and McKinsey Smith stepped out.

Instantly, unwelcome heat rose in Kate's face. To her annoyance, the memory of that night in the backyard was as powerful, as mortifying, as ever.

"The phantom boss," he said in his raspy whisper. "I was beginning to think you were a figment of my imagination." He paused, taking a moment to examine her face. "Everywhere I am, you seem to be elsewhere."

Avoiding his eyes, she moistened her lips. "I've been busy."

"You've been scared," he corrected.

"Don't be ridiculous." She began to move past him, then stopped abruptly. Now was as good a time as any to get this over with.

"I had hoped that night, I mean what happened between us that night, would just go away," she said, still without looking at him. "If I didn't mention it and you didn't mention it, we could simply forget it ever happened. But you're going to mention it, aren't you?"

"For sure."

"That's what I thought," she muttered, and turned around to face him. "Okay, let's get it out in the open. You started teasing me and it went too far." She moved her shoulders in a halfhearted shrug. "Probably because I responded so . . . so readily."

"You went up like a rocket."

Her eyes narrowed in irritation. "We're adults," she continued, her voice tight. "And we both understand human sexuality."

"I don't know." He tilted his head in a gesture that for a moment reminded her of Ben. "Sex is a pretty complicated subject. Maybe you should be more specific. Since it's obviously important to you, you wouldn't want to take a chance on being misunderstood."

"You are the most—" She broke off and forced calm into her voice. "Okay, I'll be blunt. Because I've been alone for a number of years—"

He interrupted her with a soft sound of derision. "Unless you're talking about knives, there's a distinct difference between blunt and dull. Your explanation is dull. It would be blunt to say that it's been a long time since you had your ashes hauled." His lips curved in a knowing smile. "One touch had you primed and ready."

She sucked in a sharp breath and swung around, turning her back to him, cursing the telltale heat that once again flooded her face.

When she heard movement behind her, Kate tensed, then a moment later felt his breath on the back of her neck.

"Feel the wild, sexy vibes, Kate? You called it that, remember? I liked that. And I like the way you look when you feel it."

A whisper of sound and he was even closer, his body touching hers from behind. "I could touch you right now and you'd melt. You're ready to jump out of your skin, aren't you, Katie? Just like you were that night. Know what I think? I think if I had left my knee where it was for just a little longer, you would have gone right over the edge." He gave a husky laugh. "Sweet heaven, I love it. I love knowing that I can get to you so easily."

"*Get . . . out,*" she ground out through clenched teeth.

A moment of silence; then: "Are you firing me?"

Say yes, she ordered silently. Go ahead and fire

him. Tell him to pack his things and leave. Tell him to get as far away from here as possible.

She tried. Kate really tried to get the words out, but they were stuck somewhere in the back of her throat and the only sound that came from her was a trembling little sigh.

She silently counted to ten in an attempt to relieve the tension.

"No," she said finally. "I'm not firing you. At least not now. You do a good job around here."

She moved forward a step, putting some distance between them before she turned. Still too unsettled to look at him, she stared at the floor. "But it's more than just your work. Ben—my son talks to you. He tells you things a boy can't tell his mother." Her lips twitched in a self-deprecating smile. "I was a little jealous of that at first."

Raising her head, she met his eyes. "I realize being a big brother to my son wasn't part of your job description, but I'm a good enough business-woman to like the idea of getting double for my money. So I want you to stay. As an employee and as Ben's friend. But you have to promise you'll for-get what happened . . . that night in the backyard. If you can't do that, I'll have to let you go."

Although her voice was firm and her expression determined, the threat didn't leave him shaking in his boots.

And why should it? They both knew that if she

was going to fire him, she would have done it that first day, the first time he challenged her.

In truth, and in spite of what she had just told him, Kate found the thought of his leaving vaguely disturbing.

"I won't forget," he told her now, "but I can pretend. I'll pretend it didn't happen and you can pretend it didn't happen. But it happened . . . and neither of us is going to forget it."

"I can live with that," she said, her lips curving in a slight smile. "Sometimes pretending makes it so."

"No, it doesn't," he denied softly. "If you lie to yourself often enough, you start to believe the lie. But that doesn't make it any less a lie. Somewhere inside you, the truth is still alive."

Damn the man, Kate swore silently as she moved down the hall. It was much too easy for him to get under her skin.

But, of course, it was even worse than he knew. He didn't have to say a word to her. He didn't have to be anywhere near her. All Kate had to do was think of him and her mind and body went into chaos.

Swallowing a groan, Kate looked around and suddenly realized that she was standing in the middle of the kitchen, rubbing her nose with one finger while Veda stared at her as though she had lost her mind.

"No," she said in answer to the older woman's unspoken question, "I'm not trying to communicate with extraterrestrials. I came out here to tell you that Gardner bolted, so you can save the expensive cheese for another time."

Her brow creased in thought as she began to rub tip of nose again. "As a matter of fact," she said slowly, "save it all for another time. I've just decided to take Ben to Pizza With Pizzazz for dinner." She glanced at Veda. "Want to go with us?"

"Right," the older woman said, her voice heavy with sarcasm. "Waiters dressed up in pig costumes, kids screaming in my face and throwing up on my shoes. Call me crazy, but that's not my idea of a good time."

"Mine either," Kate admitted as she turned to leave. "But to Ben, it's the next best thing to heaven."

She had almost reached the living room when she heard Mac's voice. He was in there with Ben.

Coward, she accused silently as her steps slowed, then stopped altogether. What was she going to do, hide in the closet every time she heard his voice?

"You're a natural," Mac was saying. "Oscar material, Ben. Top-notch stuff."

"In the Christmas play, I was the sad elf," Ben told him. "I had more words than the other elfs and I said them all. My mom said I was so sad, it almost made her cry. That meant I was *really* good." He paused. "Gardner said he wanted to be my father."

Kate's lips tightened in anger. Gardner Irwyn Bennett would be lucky if she didn't strangle him. He had no right to speak of such things to her son.

Moving into the doorway, Kate looked into the room, needing to see her son's expression so she could gauge the damage done by Gardner's careless words.

"But he probably needs a kid like Markie Adams," Ben continued, looking remarkably carefree as he gazed up at his friend Mac. "Markie's clothes never get dirty, and guess what he has for snacks? Carrot sticks."

Mac reacted with a husky laugh. He had one large hand resting companionably on Ben's shoulder as he stood looking down at the boy.

"Let me tell you something, Ben," he said, his voice low and slow. "Any man who was given the chance to have you for a son and didn't go down on his knees to thank God isn't much of a man."

In the shadowy hallway, Kate caught her breath. Although his voice was normal, the deep longing in Mac's smoky-gold eyes brought a swift, sharp pain to her breast.

Carefully stepping away from the door, she turned and walked away. She would wait awhile before telling Ben about the change in plans for dinner.

Mac wouldn't like knowing that Kate had seen the look on his face. He wouldn't like knowing that as she stared at him she recognized his pain and, for a moment, shared it.

And Kate didn't like knowing that her first instinct had been to go to McKinsey Smith and hold him until the pain in both of them went away.

EIGHT

"Tell Junior I'll be there as soon as I can."

Kate held the steering wheel with one hand and the phone in the other. When the car ahead moved, she eased her foot off the brake and allowed her small Chevrolet to roll forward a couple of feet.

"But if traffic doesn't pick up soon," she added wryly, "we'll be lucky if we get to that dinner in time for the mock baked Alaska."

"I'll give him the message," Veda assured her. "Just don't expect me to stay in there and entertain him until you get here. That man gives me a pain. He talks too slow. It always makes me want to smack him in the back of the head and tell him to spit it out."

Slipping off her left shoe, Kate rubbed the bottom of her aching foot on the carpet. "I would rather you didn't smack my guests unless I give a specific order. Why don't you tell Ben to keep him company?"

Pressing the button with her thumb, Kate broke the connection, dropped the phone to the seat, and reached up to rub the back of her neck with her free hand.

It had been a long day.

First thing that morning she had flown to Houston to check on the two Quick Care Centers under construction. She had spent the day on the run, talking to everyone from plumbing contractors to city council members. Then her flight back to Dallas had been delayed for over an hour. Now she was caught in a five-mile-long traffic jam.

A very long day.

And, of course, there was the Chamber of Commerce dinner yet to come.

Junior Thibideaux wasn't a member of the Chamber of Commerce. He wasn't a member of anything that had anything to do with work. But Junior had one great attribute. He was always available when Kate needed an escort.

In the past few weeks, for one reason or another, she had been forced to turn to Junior more and more often. Her other escorts seemed to have disappeared. Kate hadn't seen Peter or Julian in weeks. Douglas hadn't gotten around to returning any of the calls she had left on his machine. And Gardner hadn't put in an appearance since the day he left her house because of a stain on his jacket.

"Something my best friends won't tell me?" she muttered as traffic moved forward another few feet.

The sad part was, Kate didn't really care. She was tired of working so hard to keep her relationships with men platonic. Tired of going to party after meaningless party. Tired of being a walking advertisement for Quick Care Car Centers. She was tired, period.

A strange thought had come to her on the flight home: She could sell out.

Even to consider selling her business was a little scary, but the more Kate thought about it, the more she was drawn to the idea. She could put part of her profit into stocks or real estate, whatever secure arena Peter Allbright recommended, and use the rest to start another venture, something that would give her some real satisfaction.

And what would do that? she wondered.

"What do I want to be when I grow up?" she murmured aloud.

It wasn't a new question. In high school and later in college, it had bothered Kate that all her friends were so definite about what they wanted to do with their lives. Out of a bottomless grab bag, they had pulled career choices. Teacher. Doctor. Lawyer. Engineer. But for Kate it was different. She hadn't had a clue. She only knew that she wanted to feel passionate about her life's work.

And now, years later, she still wanted that. And she still had no idea what to choose.

Thirty minutes later, when Kate opened the backdoor and walked into the kitchen, the only conclusion she had reached was that she was too tired to reach a conclusion.

A few feet into the room she paused. Mac was there. At least the bottom half of him was. He was lying on his back under the sink, one knee raised. His lower body was twisted slightly, all his muscles tight.

Kate was tired. That was why she didn't have the strength to look away from his body. That was why she wasn't able to ignore the little electric zing that was caroming around her lower regions.

Almost a month had passed since the night they met in the backyard. After their little talk, Mac had managed to observe all the proprieties. Although there was occasionally a certain look in his eyes or a trace of something in his husky voice that told her he wasn't going to forget what happened between them that night, so far he had kept his word and hadn't mentioned it again.

Now, as she laid her briefcase on the counter, he slid out from under the sink, rested the wrench in his hands on his stomach, and looked up at her. "The disposal was making funny noises," he explained.

"Veda was probably trying to grind up someone

who annoyed her." She glanced around. "Speaking of our little ray of sunshine, where is she?"

Reaching back under the sink, he gave something one last twist. "The butcher sent the wrong cuts of meat for your party tomorrow night, so she decided to go yell at him in person. I gather this is a long-standing feud."

"It's sort of a love-hate relationship." She stretched her neck to one side then the other, trying to work out a kink. "Veda hates the butcher and loves to yell."

He sat up and examined her face as he wiped his hands on a rag. A moment later he rose to his feet, walked to the refrigerator, and pulled out a bottle of mineral water. After twisting off the cap, he handed it to her.

"Thanks." Kate took a long swallow, then held the cold bottle to one temple as she leaned back against the counter. "What do you think about art galleries?"

One eyebrow quirked in surprise. "Let's see," he said slowly. "The lighting is generally pretty good, but the people who spend a lot of time there always talk funny. When you go to a special exhibition, get there early or all the food will be gone. Steer clear of people who are trying to find something to match the sofa. Don't ask the opinion of a serious collector or you'll be stuck all night." He paused and glanced at her. "How am I doing?"

She laughed and shook her head. "I meant as a business proposition. No, never mind. That's not really what I want to do anyway."

He raised one brow. "Don't tell me you're thinking of adding to the empire."

"Not adding. Swapping." She took another long swallow of cold water. "I'm going to tell you a secret, Mac, but if you repeat it, I'll swear you're lying."

"My lips are sealed." His honey-gold eyes gleamed with humor as he crossed his heart with one finger. "Honor of a handyman."

She leaned closer and lowered her voice. "I don't care whether or not cars get dirty."

Drawing in a slow breath, she moved a couple of steps away from him, and as she continued, her words gained strength and momentum.

"It's just not an important issue in my life. Sometimes . . . sometimes when I'm meeting with a company rep who's trying to sell me new improved hot wax, or some marketing genius who wants to map out an advertising campaign guaranteed to capture the interest of the car-washing public, I sit there and listen to them talking so earnestly, a light burning in their eyes, a quivering fervor— that can only be described as religious—in their voices, and I feel an overwhelming urge to grab them by the collars and say, 'Get a grip, people. We're talking about *car washes*.' "

He had been laughing through most of her diatribe. Now he shook his head. "They wouldn't get your point."

"I know, and that makes it worse."

Rubbing his chin with one finger, he studied her face. "Instead of buying a gallery, why don't you create something to hang in one?"

Kate frowned. She used to paint. A long, long time ago. Several people had even told her that her paintings were good. David, because he loved her, had given her talent an importance she personally doubted it deserved. Back then she had been too unsure of herself to let anyone other than her husband see her work.

Maybe—

She shot a sharp glance at Mac. "What makes you think I have artistic abilities?"

He shrugged. "I don't know. Your hands, I guess. They look like artist's hands."

Frowning, she dropped her gaze to her hands. They were ordinary hands. The right number of fingers, opposable thumbs, medium-length nails. Ordinary.

"You look tired," he said, abruptly interrupting her thoughts.

When she raised her head and found him watching her, she smiled. "Good guess." Leaning back against the counter with a weary sigh, she glanced over her shoulder toward the front of the house. "Is my escort still waiting, or did he get fed up and go home?"

"He's still here." He tilted his head to one side, his lips curving in a wry smile. "You know, Junior's lucky he's rich. He's not exactly a top mental specimen, is he?"

"If you're trying to get me riled, it won't work. I'm too tired to take offense. Junior's okay."

"Probably real restful."

His oblique indictment startled a laugh out of her. "As a matter of fact, he is."

Moving closer, he let his gaze drift over her face again. "You're ready to fall asleep on your feet," he said, his voice low and husky. "Why don't you cancel your date and spend a couple of hours soaking in a hot tub?"

"Don't tempt me," she groaned, then pushed away from the counter. "I can't do it. I have to go to this dinner. Make contacts. Schmooze a little."

As she walked to the door she added, "A shower massage, a few dabs of witch hazel, and I'll be good as new."

It was a lie, but Kate was going to do her level best to make it so.

As she reached the staircase she could hear her son talking to Junior, evidently entertaining her date as Kate had requested. She must have been subconsciously taking in the conversation because a moment later she stopped abruptly and frowned.

Turning around, she walked back down the stairs and moved closer to the living-room door.

" . . . and she says having really lots of money is a bad thing. She says if she ever got really lots of money, she would give it all away. She'd just give it away."

"What? What were you saying?"

"I was just talking 'bout how my mom would give the money away. And maybe if she got a husband, she would make him give it away too. You have really lots of money . . . don't you, Junior?"

"Well, yes . . . yes, I guess I do."

"But you wouldn't mind not having any, would you? I mean, you could get a job and everything."

"Job? What kind of job? Why should I get a job?"

"Well . . . but maybe you wouldn't have to. If my mom gave all the money away like she said, we could probably just be tramps. I saw a movie about tramps. They kept a spoon in their pocket so they could eat right out of the can. It was beans. Do you think there's a rule that says tramps can just only eat beans? And they slept on the ground under a tree in the park. I'd like to sleep on the ground, wouldn't you, Junior? If you married my mom and she made you give all your money away, we could make it like a camping trip. And every day we could—"

"I think we've heard quite enough from you, mister," Kate said as she walked into the room.

On the couch, Junior was leaning forward, per-spiration covering his smooth forehead. Kate almost laughed at the naked horror in his eyes.

With her hands on her hips, she stood looking down at her son. "Would you like to tell me what's going on?"

Ben shrugged. "Me and Junior was just talk-ing."

"Junior and I were just talking," she corrected. "Yes, I gathered that much. And from what I heard, you were doing most of the talking. Why are you making up stories about being a tramp and living in the park?"

"It wasn't a story, least not really. 'Member that time on 'Life of the Rich and Famous,' and that guy's house was so big he had to drive to get to the other end, and you said it was bad for him to have so much money, and if you had that much money, you'd just give it away? 'Member that?"

"I couldn't give my money away," Junior said, his voice weak. "It's in a trust fund. I don't have the power to—sleeping under a tree, on the ground, out in the open . . . Kate, that's *dangerous*. Besides, I've always had a weak chest and the dampness—"

"Junior . . . *Junior*." When she was sure she had his attention, she said slowly and firmly: "No one wants you to sleep under a tree."

Turning her head, she sent her son an evil look. "Ben was just being cute. And now he's going to go to his room and sit in the corner in his thinking chair and give some thought to what happens to little boys who get too cute."

Turning her head, she smiled at her date. "I promise I won't keep you waiting much longer."

Poor Junior, she thought, hiding a smile as she pointed Ben in the direction of the stairs. Being a member of the idle rich was Junior's one and only source of pride. It was a wonder he hadn't run screaming from the house. Ben had picked the one thing guaranteed to unsettle him.

At the foot of the stairs, she stopped and frowned. *How* had he managed to pick that one thing?

Rubbing the tip of her nose with one finger, she began to sort through the events of the past few weeks. Gardner had left the house in a panic, immediately after talking to Ben. Julian. Peter. Douglas. All of them had been regular escorts and all of them had disappeared without a word. At least, without a word to *her*.

Something was going on, and whatever it was, there was no way Ben had come up with it on his own.

But Kate was pretty sure she knew who had.

Swinging around abruptly, she headed back toward the kitchen.

Veda, in the process of unpacking a box of steaks, glanced up when Kate walked in. "So you finally got out of the traffic jam."

"Finally," Kate said, her gaze firmly on Mac.

He raised one dark brow in inquiry, and when she continued to stare in silence, he said, "Well, I guess I'll mosey along. The disposal seems to be all right now, but if it starts making funny noises again, you may want to think about getting a new one."

Still silent, Kate waited for him to leave, then followed him into the backyard.

When the screen slammed behind her, he turned around. "I thought maybe you had something you wanted to say to Veda in private. I guess I was wrong."

"I guess you were."

He stood for a moment, hands in pockets, then a slight smile twitched at his lips. "Was there something you wanted to talk to me about?"

"Oh, yes." The words were clipped, her stance openly hostile. "Oh yes, I definitely want to talk to you about something." She drew in a slow breath. "I was on my way upstairs when I happened to over-hear a conversation between my son and my date."

He shook his head slowly in regret. "Eavesdropping? Is that polite?"

"Do you know what Ben was doing in there?" she asked then rolled her eyes. "Why am I asking? Of course you know. He was entertaining my date with tales of what it will be like to be a bum, after Junior marries me and I make him give away all his money."

That this brought an appreciative laugh from Mac made her eyes narrow in anger. "At first I wondered if Veda was behind it, but this isn't Veda's style. You put him up to it, didn't you?"

"Put him up to it?" He shook his head. "No, I'm afraid I can't take that much credit. Ben came to me with a problem and I gave him a little advice."

"This is unforgivable. Absolutely unforgivable." She walked a few steps away, then swung around and walked back. "I know that tormenting me gives you some kind of secret thrill, but how could you use Ben like this?"

"I wasn't using him," he said quietly. "I was helping him."

"What on earth made you think—" She stopped to draw in another calming breath. "Explain yourself, please."

He stared down at the ground for a moment, then glanced up and met her gaze squarely. "It started the day Bennett was here. I was in the basement when Ben came down. He admitted he was hiding again and told me why." He shrugged. "Eventually we got around to discussing all of your men. It seems that Ben was worried you would marry one of them."

"Oh, please," she said, throwing up her hands in exasperation. "You can come up with a better story than that. Ben couldn't possibly—"

"You weren't there." His voice was quiet but

firm. "You didn't see the look on his face. The boy was scared."

"Scared? But why—" She broke off, her thoughts confused. "I just assumed he knew—"

"You can't assume," he interrupted, and now she heard the fierce intensity in his voice. "When it concerns Ben, you have to know for sure."

Although Kate tried, she found she couldn't resent him for telling her how to deal with her own son. Whatever else she thought about McKinsey Smith, she knew he genuinely cared for Ben.

She exhaled a slow, weary breath. "If Ben was really worried like you said, why didn't he come to me? Why didn't he tell me how he felt?"

"He was afraid it would hurt your feelings."

This brought a startled laugh from her. "My son always manages to surprise me," she said, shaking her head. "He didn't have anything to worry about. I never thought of marrying any of the men I date."

By unspoken agreement, they began to walk together. "They're all good friends," she went on, "but even if they had been more than friends, I wouldn't have considered it. None of them clicked with Ben. I would never marry anyone who didn't have a special feeling for my son."

"Bobby Sherwood's father has a special feeling for your son," he said after a moment. "From what Ben told me, I would say they get along real well."

"I'll bet." She gave her head a slight, irresolute shake. "No, it has to be right for me as well. I don't mean that I have to be desperately in love with the man I marry—if and when I ever remarry—but I do need to like him. I need to care about him."

He glanced sideways at her. "Looks like being a parent can get complicated."

"You said a mouthful," she said, her voice rueful. "Some little thing happens and you start to wonder if it's really a little thing after all. Maybe, to your child, it's something important. Maybe it's something that will affect the rest of his life."

Her steps slowed and she raised her head to meet his eyes. "Me," she said in a low whisper. "That's it. That's all Ben has. You have this wonderful little life, and I'm *totally* responsible." She tapped her chest with the knuckle of her index finger. "I'm the one who has to keep him healthy and strong. I have to make sure he's happy and secure. It's all up to me . . . and frankly that scares the pants off me."

"Understandable. But if you remarried, you would be able to share the load."

"Share?" She made a wry face. "With whom? Junior?"

"Not hardly," he said with a short laugh. "But there are other men around."

"I know. And some of them are good uns, as Ben would say. But how can I be sure which one will put Ben's welfare above his own? I haven't found that kind of man yet. I'm not even sure he exists."

But he does, she thought suddenly. The man beside her would put her son's welfare first. Strange that she should be so sure of that. But she was just as certain that it was a truth that would be better left unsaid.

Moving to stand in front of her, he stared down at her for a long, silent moment. "It's been tough on you, hasn't it? Not just raising him on your own, but worrying about him on your own as well."

"That's the worst part." She gave a soft, rueful laugh. "Lying awake at night, terrified that I'll do something wrong. Little fears grow in the dark, you know. And there's no one there to say, 'Lighten up. You're making too much out of nothing.'"

He laid one rough palm against her cheek. "I'm sorry," he said in his raspy whisper. "I'm sorry you've had to do it all alone."

Mac's words didn't quite reach her. She was too taken up by the sound of his voice, the intensity in his eyes, and the way his warm hand felt on her face.

"You're not really so tough, are you, Kate?"

Her lips moved in an unsteady smile. "Why don't we let that be our little secret? Pretense is the glue that holds me together. If I ever stopped pretending, I don't know what would happen. I would probably spend all my time hiding in the closet."

When he didn't respond, when he simply stood there, his body only inches away from hers as he stared into her eyes, Kate felt her pulse quicken in anticipation of . . . of what?

"Well . . ." She paused and cleared her throat. "I guess I'd better get back inside. If I hurry, we may have time to make that dinner after all."

"You mean Junior's still hanging in there?" His lips twitched in a crooked smile. "I was afraid it would take more to move him than it did the others. Something along the lines of a dirt hauler."

"Leave Junior alone," she said, returning his smile. "Thanks to you and Ben, it looks like he's going to be my main man for a while."

The change in Mac was instant and complete. His eyes narrowed, his features grew hard, and when he spoke, his voice had taken on a sarcastic edge. "Until you can cultivate a new crop, that is."

And then he turned and walked away from her without another word.

"Back to normal," Kate murmured as she slowly made her way back to the house.

Just for a moment something had been different.

For one brief moment, when Mac's hand was on her face and he was staring down into her eyes, Kate could have sworn she saw the same look of painful longing that was sometimes there when he looked at her son.

NINE

"I feel like a damned sneak," Ralph grumbled. "I hate having to wait until I know Kate's not here before I come to see you or Ben."

The two men were in the garage apartment. Ralph talked and paced while David ate his lunch at the bar that separated the kitchen from the small living room. Kate had left a few minutes earlier for a business meeting.

David picked up his sandwich and took a bite. "If it makes you feel uncomfortable, don't do it."

The older man threw him a disgruntled look, then exhaled a noisy sigh. "I'm afraid to come around when she's home. I'm afraid I'll screw up and say something stupid and make things worse than they already are. Every time she calls me, she always ends up asking if anything's wrong, if there's something she can do to help. *She's* worried about *me*. Do you believe that?" He shook his head. "I keep telling her everything is just fine, but she knows damned well I'm lying because she starts asking questions about my health, my business, my love life."

David glanced over his shoulder, one brow raised. "You still have a love life?"

"Not that it's any of your business, but yes, I do."

"You ought to settle down." David's lips curved in a wicked smile. "As a matter of fact, I know who would be perfect for you. Veda."

"That virago? Do you really think I'm going to get hooked up with someone who would most likely kill me in my sleep after the first argument?" The older man grinned sheepishly. "Besides, she won't go out with me. She says I remind her of her first husband."

David laughed. "From what I've heard of Trip LaSalle, you can probably take that as a compliment. She said he was the sexiest thing alive."

Ralph cocked his head in speculation. "Do you think—" Breaking off, he shoved his hands in his pockets. "Stop trying to change the subject. We're supposed to be talking about you." He paused and moved closer. "I'm worried about you, son. I'm worried about Kate and Ben, too, but mostly I'm worried about you."

David gave a short laugh. "I've recently discovered that worrying is what parents do best."

"How long do you think you can keep this up?"

Ralph's voice and expression showed genuine concern. "You're digging the hole deeper and deeper every day."

Turning his back on his friend, David put down his iced-tea glass and stared at the wall. What was he supposed to say to that? He wasn't sure of anything anymore. How could he tell Ralph what he was going to do or how he felt, when he didn't know himself? He didn't even know how he *should* feel.

After some heavy soul-searching, David had finally acknowledged the fact that he had used the situation with Ben to his own advantage. It would have been very easy to have gone to Kate and told her that Ben was worried about having a stepfather. She would have known exactly what to say to the boy to reassure him, to make him feel secure.

But that wasn't the way David wanted it to happen. He had wanted Ben's problem solved, but *he* wanted to be the one to solve it. He had needed to be important to his son.

But, of course, that wasn't the only motive behind his actions. There was something else, as strong as his desire to help his son but not as easily defined. David had wanted, he had *needed*, to send Kate's men packing. He didn't want a single one of them around her. Not even slow-talking, slow-thinking Junior.

Feeling more harassed by his own emotions than by Ralph's questions, he rose abruptly to his feet.

"It's getting a little complicated," he murmured, his lips twisting in a rueful smile.

The older man responded with a loud, expressive snort. "A little complicated, you say? That's like saying hell's just a tad hot."

Moving a step closer, Ralph reached out and laid one large hand on David's shoulder. "You have to do what you think is right, boy. And I'd be the last one to tell you just exactly what right is. But sooner or later, one way or another, the truth is going to come out. And when it does, I don't want any of you—you, Kate, or Ben—to get hurt by it."

An hour later, as David trimmed the small hedge that lined the driveway, he found his thoughts returning again and again to the conversation with Ralph.

The old geezer was right. As long as David stayed here, as long as he was so involved with their lives, there was a chance the truth would come out by accident. The only way to retain control, the only way to make certain that his identity would be revealed when and how he thought best for everyone, was for him to leave.

And that was something David couldn't do. Not now. Not yet.

If he could somehow manage to examine his feelings for Kate rationally, maybe other things would become clear as well. Maybe he would be able to understand why he was still here, holding fast to the status quo. If he knew that, then maybe he could figure out what the hell he was going to do next.

A moment later he heard the backdoor slam and suddenly Ben was beside him, pulling at David's arm as he hopped up and down in excitement.

"Mac . . . Mac, it's a *'mergency*! I forgot to tell my mom there's a game today. But it's not just a reg'lar game. If we win, we'll be champions of the whole districk. I'm the best batter on my team. They *need* me, Mac. Come on . . . come on, we gotta hurry." Grasping David's hand, he began to tug at it urgently. "Coach said we have to be there at three and it's already two and four-oh." He held out his wrist, showing David the face of the plastic digital watch.

"You're right. It's definitely two and four-oh, but why are you telling me?" Rising to his feet, David glanced toward the house. "Where's Veda?"

The boy was hopping up and down again. "She can't go. She has to wait for somebody to bring her new barking lounge chair that leans back and jiggles. But you could take me. You'd like that, wouldn't you, Mac?"

"Sure thing." He frowned, rubbing his jaw as

he allowed his son to lead him a couple of steps in the direction of his car. "But don't you think maybe we'd better check and make sure this is all right with your mother?"

"I already called her on the car phone. She says I can ask you, but if you don't want to, I can't whine or look pitiful at you." He stopped for a moment and glanced up at David. "But you really want to, don't you, Mac, and that's not even whining."

David chuckled. "It's not whining, but I'm afraid you look pretty pitiful. Okay, sport, give me a couple of minutes to clean up and we'll go."

The sports park where the game was to be held had been a big open field until the city divided it up into playing fields. The park contained six soccer fields as well as six baseball diamonds, each enclosed by chain-link fences. Hundreds of cars were parked on the grass around the fields, following an orderless pattern apparently set by the first cars to arrive. The portable refreshment stands that had been brought in for the day's events offered snow cones, popcorn, cold drinks, and dill pickles of gargantuan size. Two sets of small bleachers were positioned near each playing field, but most of the spectators had brought folding lawn chairs and sat at the edge of the soccer fields or right up against the chain-link fences in order to give their offspring instruction and encouragement as the game progressed.

When David and Ben arrived at the park, the opposing team was using the field to practice. Ben's team, the Badgers, would take their turn next.

Although the temperature had only reached the mideighties, the lack of clouds or any significant breeze made it seem warmer. As they walked toward the bull pen David shrugged out of the windbreaker he had worn over a navy T-shirt.

Ben glanced up at his arms. "You don't have as much scars on your arms as you do on your back." He paused. "I guess you probably had a lot of fights."

David's lips quirked in a sardonic smile. "One-sided fights," he acknowledged.

"How do you do a one-sided fight?"

"It's not that hard," he murmured. "There are people in the world who like to cause pain, especially to someone who can't fight back." He glanced down and met his son's eyes. "Don't ever do that, Ben. Don't ever fight someone who can't give you a fair fight."

The boy nodded solemnly. "There's this kid, Malcolm, he has wires on his leg to make it grow straight. One time a fourth grader came up and started pushing him around and stuff. And I got in trouble with Miss Evans for throwing dirt at him— the fourth grader, not Malcolm—and callin' him a stupid butt."

"You threw dirt at him?"

Ben grinned. "That way I didn't have to get close enough for him to hit me. He was *big*." He paused, his brown eyes squinting in concentration. "See, the best thing about being in a fight is so you can tell your friends about it. If you say you threw dirt at a kid in the fourth grade, or you clobbered Big Roy Gene—he's the meanest kid in the whole second grade—that would be something good to tell. But it would sound pretty dumb saying you won a fight with a kid that's got wires on his leg."

David stared down at him, his heart swelling, filling up with pride. And he found himself silently thanking Kate. She had done a fine job of raising this boy. No man could ask for a better son.

A second later, when Ben's friends spotted him and began to shout for him to hurry up, David walked to the small bleacher nearest the Badgers' bull pen. Finding an empty spot on the end, he sat down and listened to the pep talk the coach was giving the boys.

After a while he became aware of the people occupying the seats around him, sensing the care they were taking not to look directly at the deep scars on his arms.

"You're with Ben Moore?"

Turning his head, he found that the woman next to him was not as discreet as the others on the stands. She was staring at him in open curiosity. Automatically, David didn't like her. The speculation in her eyes was the nasty kind. Hiding a smile, he wondered if she was Big Roy Gene's mother.

He nodded. "Yes, I'm with Ben."

"I guess Kate couldn't make it today." She shook her head in regret. "Some people simply don't understand that children are more important than business." She paused for his response. When he gave none, her lips tightened and she said, "Are you a relative? Ben's uncle?"

"I'm a friend," he said, his voice quiet and husky.

"A friend," she repeated. "Do you mean a friend of Kate's or—"

At that moment the attention of everyone in the vicinity was drawn to the Badgers' bull pen. The boys were clumped together in the center. Someone shouted, "Fight! Fight!" while one lone voice was just as clearly yelling, "Get up, Ben! Hit 'im again!"

Even though most of the parents left the bleacher at a run, David was the first to enter the narrow enclosure. He didn't immediately see Ben, but he quickly picked out his son's opponent, a boy who was taller and wider than the others.

Reaching into the tangle of excited youth, he located and slowly began to extract his son. When he turned with the wriggling boy under his arm, he almost tripped over the nosy woman who had been sitting beside him earlier.

She was on her knees beside the other pugilist, and now she shot a venomous glance up at David. "If you're going to be in charge of your little *friend*," she spat out, "you'd better damned well learn how to control him. Just look what he did to my Sonny."

Ignoring her, David carried Ben out of the bull pen and away from the crowd. When they were several feet from the baseball field, he set the boy on his feet and studied his face. It was still red with fury, his small fingers still clenched into fists.

"Calm down . . . come on, Ben, it's over." Resting both hands on Ben's shoulders, he looked into the boy's eyes. "Now, you want to tell me what that was all about?"

"I showed my friends where you were sitting and told them you were my best friend now." The words were tight with anger and slightly breathless, his thin chest rising and falling rapidly. "Chad said the scars on your arms made you look like a Ninja warrior. Then Sonny Boosier, who is nothin' but a *big ol' snot*, said the scars made you look deformed. And . . . and that's why I said Sonny's face makes him look like a geeky turd."

David pressed his lips together, controlling the urge to laugh. "And that's when the fight started?"

Ben shook his head. "No, then Sonny said how'd you get the scars anyway, and I told him you got them from ripping the heads off geeky turds. *That's* when the fight started. Sonny pushed me into Jeremy, and Jeremy pushed me back into Sonny." He shrugged. "I got tired of getting pushed, so I punched Sonny in the stomach." He glanced up at David. "Sonny Boosier sure is squishy."

David cleared his throat and somehow managed to keep a straight face as he said, "I'm afraid your people skills need a little work."

Keeping a hand on the boy's shoulder, he went down on one knee. "Listen to me, son. This next part's not going to be easy. I want you to go back over there and tell Sonny you're sorry you called him a geeky turd."

"But, Mac—"

David shook his head. "No buts. This is what you have to do. Because you're a good kid. And because you're strong. Strong enough to handle the tough things. I know Sonny was rude, but that doesn't matter." He kept his gaze steadily on the boy's small face. "You see, Ben, you can't make Sonny stop doing wrong things. You can only make sure that what you do is right. Understand?"

Ben didn't answer right away. He swung around and kicked at the dirt. He punched the palm of his hand with his fist a couple of times. Then he drew in a deep breath, his upper body rising in the process.

"Well . . . well, I'm not sorry I called him that. Sonny *is* a geeky turd and everybody in the whole second grade knows it." He turned his head and looked back at the field. "But I'll go over there and say it, even if it is a big ol' lie. But it's only 'cause you told me to."

David followed along behind him and stood near the enclosed pen as Ben went back in. Sonny's mother was still there, standing close to her son, shooting venomous looks at both Ben and David as the former began to speak.

Ben's words were low and they all ran together, but it was nonetheless an apology. The look of satisfaction in Sonny's eyes made David want to smack him, and the boy offered no apology in return, nor did his mother demand one. It was some consolation that the other boys avoided Sonny and each reached over to give Ben a sympathetic pat on the back.

When the adults returned to their seats, Mrs. Boosier decided to sit at the other end of the stands. Another consolation.

A quarter of an hour later, when Ben left the pen to take his place in the batter's box, a circle on the ground that indicated he was next in line to bat, the boy's expression was still moody, and David hoped that once he got into the game, he would forget about the fight and his squishy adversary.

❦————————❦

"There are a couple of other things I need to talk to you about while you're here," O'Halloran said.

Kate sat in a chair across the desk from Kevin O'Halloran, a feasibility expert and troubleshooter whom she used occasionally. His office was in one of the high-gloss, high-priced, high-rise buildings that lined the freeways in north Dallas. Kate had been there for almost an hour, and she still hadn't managed to work up any enthusiasm for the project under discussion.

"First, the Midland–Odessa sites you were considering." He pulled several papers from a stack. "Apparently, word leaked out that you're a prospective buyer and, well, I don't have to tell you what that means. I have a couple of alternate sites that I'd like to show you. This one, as you can see . . ."

Kate leaned forward in her chair to accept the paper, arranging her features to simulate interest.

She simply didn't care anymore. Maybe it was heartless of her, but she didn't care that all the dust in west Texas made it imperative for the people who lived there to have access to quality car washes.

She wished she had canceled this meeting and gone to Ben's ball game instead. It was only the second game she had missed, but she didn't like her work coming between her and her son even to that limited degree.

A small smile twitched at her lips. She had only this moment realized that knowing Mac was with Ben somehow made her feel better, less like a negligent parent. Mac would know how to show the proper amount of encouragement and enthusiasm. She could count on Mac.

When the phone on O'Halloran's desk rang, he picked it up and then shot a glance at Kate. "Yes, she's still here," he said, then handed Kate the receiver.

"It's me."

Kate recognized the husky voice immediately. Her heart gave one sharp thump of fear as she rose to her feet. "What is it? Is Ben—"

"A bat hit him in the head," Mac told her, his tone calm. "He seems okay, but I thought I should get him checked over by a doctor. We're at West Park Hospital now."

"Thanks for calling." Even though her thoughts were frantic, she kept her voice as even as his had been. "I'm on my way."

Half an hour later Kate walked into West Park Hospital through the emergency entrance. Apparently Mac had been watching for her because he was beside her before she had a chance to get her bearings.

"They just took him down to be X-rayed," he told her.

"But he's okay?" She searched his eyes for reassurance. "I mean, you did say he was all right?"

He nodded. "He was disoriented for a few seconds immediately after the bat hit him, then he seemed the same as always. He didn't even have a headache." He glanced away, his features tightening. "But it was a solid hit."

"I don't understand how he could have been hit by a bat." Kate raked an unsteady hand across her face. "Unless— Was he standing behind someone taking practice swings?"

Still avoiding her eyes, Mac shoved his hands in his back pockets and shook his head. "Ben was next in line to bat. The boy ahead of him got a hit, something that apparently doesn't happen very often. He got a little excited and slung the bat. It was just bad luck that he slung it directly at Ben."

Kate didn't respond immediately. Puzzled, she took a moment to examine his features, trying to decipher his mood. "There's something you're not telling me."

"The whole stupid thing was my fault." His voice was low and intense to the point of curtness. "He wasn't paying attention. He would have seen it coming if he hadn't been distracted."

He raised his head to meet her eyes. "A few minutes before the game started, he was in a fight. A kid named Sonny was making fun of the scars on my arms and—"

"—and Ben punched him," she finished for him. Kate knew her son. Defender of the underdog. Champion of the forgotten. "I still don't see how that makes it your fault."

"There wouldn't have been a fight if I hadn't been—"

"If you hadn't been you?" she asked, her voice soft with understanding. "Don't be stupid. It wasn't your fault. It wasn't even Sonny's, even though he's the most obnoxious kid on the face of the earth. Ben could just as easily have been distracted by a butterfly or a funny-looking cloud. That's just the way he is."

He shook his head in contradiction. "You don't understand. I handled it all wrong. I made him apologize, even though the other kid started it." His face twisted with anguish. "Dear God, if anything happens to him—"

She placed a hand on his upper arm, gripping it, stopping him from finishing the thought. "Nothing's going to happen to him."

Kate suddenly remembered having had the feeling that he had lost a child. Something like that would make Ben's accident seem even more scary than it was in reality.

"I think I know what you're feeling now," she said, choosing her words carefully. "When you . . . when you suffer a loss, it makes you too aware that tragedy isn't reserved for the other guy. Suddenly you realize that it can happen to you too."

She paused, examining his smoky eyes to see if her words were having any effect. "I think maybe you've lost someone you love, and now, because you've come to care about Ben, you almost feel like your love is a jinx."

He leaned his head back and exhaled a slow breath. "Yes, I've lost people I loved," he said in a rough whisper. "It almost puts you off loving, doesn't it?"

"Almost."

She gave her head a little shake. It was funny how helping him through the crisis had kept her from going crazy with fear. A shared worry made the burden lighter.

Sensing that he had gained a measure of control, Kate decided it was time to change the subject.

"How *did* you get those scars?" she asked.

His lips twitched in a slight smile. "Pulling the heads off geeky turds."

She chuckled. "That sounds like Ben's version . . . and if I catch him using that T-word again, I promise he will live to regret it." She paused. "Were you in an accident?"

Glancing away from her, he shook his head. "Some people with chips on their shoulders decided to take their bad mood out on me."

"Someone did that to you deliberately?"

He gave a short laugh. "Oh yes, they were very deliberate. And thorough. The scars on my arms are nothing to what's on my back."

Deliberate? Thorough? What—

She dropped her gaze to his right arm, then a moment later caught her breath sharply. "Torture?" she whispered in horrified disbelief. "Are you talking about torture? But why? What on earth could have provoked something so . . . so outrageously *evil*?"

He turned and began to move toward a line of chairs. "I guess you could say I wandered onto their turf." Kate thought she detected a note of dry humor in his voice. "Some people are very territorial."

"A gang?" She sat next to him in one of the gray plastic chairs, her body turned toward him. "Here in Dallas?"

"No, not here."

"But—" She broke off and frowned. "I guess I always thought of gangs as hoods who attacked people in alleys or drove by to shoot at members of other gangs. I've never heard of them torturing their victims."

He leaned his head back against the wall. "Who

knows what evil lurks in the heart of man?" he said in a husky whisper.

She glanced down at her hands, then back at him. "Can you talk about it?"

"I can, but why should I?" He shrugged. "It's over."

"Is it? Were they caught? Were they punished for what they did?" When he shook his head, she said, "Then it's not over. Especially if you can't talk about it. You're still carrying it all around with you."

Although he didn't respond, the muscle beside his mouth twitched a couple of times before he tightened his lips. Whatever had happened to him was obviously still eating at him. And why shouldn't it? No one could go through that kind of thing and come out unscathed.

"If you don't want to talk to me," she said quietly, "there are professionals who could—"

"A shrink?" he interrupted, shaking his head. "No thank you. I'll handle it my own way. I'm doing just fine without having to—"

He broke off abruptly, his eyes narrowing as he gazed at a point beyond her. Suddenly he was on his feet, taking her arm, pulling her forward to introduce her to a small dark woman, the doctor who had examined Ben.

"I've looked at the X rays," Dr. Weisman told them, her eyes sparkling, her full lips curving in an understanding smile. "Your son is fine. Better than fine. That Ben's a real character. And fortunately he has a nice hard head."

Kate didn't know until that moment exactly how frightened she had been. Relief left her momentarily weak and she glanced at Mac, needing to share her happiness.

Sensing her movement, he swung around abruptly and walked a couple of steps away from her. But he hadn't moved soon enough. She had already seen the glistening of tears in those smoky-gold eyes.

Following him, she moved to stand in front of him. After a moment she reached up and rested the palm of her hand on his face. "Didn't I tell you he'd be all right?" she whispered with an unsteady smile.

He sucked in a sharp breath and his features twisted with emotion as he pulled her into his arms, held her tightly against him.

Kate had known for a long time that he cared for her son, but only now did she realize just how much Ben meant to him.

Mac loved Ben. He really loved him.

But there was more than overwhelming relief in the way he was holding her, she realized. It was almost as though he were afraid to let her go.

Puzzled, she pulled back slightly to examine his features, but already he was releasing her and turning to the doctor, who was patiently waiting to take them to Ben.

As they walked together down the hall Kate kept glancing at Mac, thinking of the intensity of his reactions, understanding and accepting the depth of his feelings for her son. In only three months he had—

She stopped abruptly, her eyes widening as she sucked in a sharp breath.

When Mac glanced at her in inquiry, she avoided his eyes and forced herself to start moving again. But as they followed Dr. Weisman down the hall, her thoughts were chaotic, almost hysterical.

As crazy as it seemed, as unbelievable, in thinking of how lucky Ben was to have the love of a man like Mac, Kate had recognized in herself an empty little ache. A twinge of wistful longing. A secret wish that this man's caring might extend to her as well.

Dear Lord, she thought, moistening her dry lips, was it possible?

Either Kate was going out of her mind or she was actually beginning to fall in love with the mysterious, incredibly complicated man who walked beside her.

TEN

" . . . and after that we're going to play *three* video games 'cause Chad's mom lets him stay up till *'leven* when he has sleepover friends."

Ben was talking nonstop as he walked toward the car parked at the curb. The yellow vinyl backpack strapped to his back was full to overflowing and bulged with mysterious bumps and lumps. Kate had checked it earlier, and although there was actually a change of clothing inside, most of the bulk came from toys and games, things Ben had decided he and Chad couldn't do without on this overnight visit.

After speaking briefly to Chad's mother, Kate stood on the sidewalk and watched them drive away, waving until the car was out of sight. And even before it turned the corner, she missed Ben.

Three days had passed since the accident and she

had spent most of those three days doing "together" things with her son. They made cookies. They played video games. They watched endless cartoons. And at night, she would go into his bedroom to stand beside his bed and watch him sleep.

Now, as she walked slowly back to the house, Kate's lips twisted in a wry smile. She had been a mother long enough to know that eventually everything would return to normal and she would once again think longingly of the unenlightened days when children were repressed but blessedly silent. But for a while yet she would let her son get away with murder simply because he had come away from the accident with nothing more than a good story to tell his friends.

In her office, she switched on her computer and settled down at her desk. She would use this time to catch up on her work and would take her mind off the strange stillness her son's absence always brought to the house.

Two hours later Kate was still sitting at her desk. Her hair was ruffled from having restless fingers drawn through it too many times as she tried to force herself to concentrate on the work at hand.

With a soft sound of exasperation, she pushed back her chair and rose abruptly to her feet. The twitchy restlessness that wouldn't go away and wouldn't let her relax was more than wishing Ben was here so she could keep an eye on him. And it was more than being disenchanted with her work. She knew exactly what was wrong with her. But she didn't have a clue as to what she was supposed to do about it.

Swinging around on her heel, she left her office and walked to the living room. Except for the flickering light from the television, the room was dark.

Veda, in an ancient velour robe, was curled up on the couch with a bowl of buttered popcorn beside her. She glanced up when Kate walked in.

"*TV Times* lied," the older woman said in disgust. "*Backstreet*, the best crying movie ever made, was supposed to be on now." She waved a hand at the screen. "Even if you put all the hacked-up body parts back together, that broad could never look like Susan Hayward." She heaved a noisy sigh. "Gushing blood and decomposing bodies. When I was a kid, they didn't allow gore in horror movies. Remember when we thought Godzilla was scary?"

"Godzilla was never scary," Kate said, her voice distracted. "He was big and clumsy and loud. And totally unbelievable."

"Well, that's my point. Godzilla scared me. Teen slasher movies like this one scared you. It makes you wonder what they'll have to come up with to scare Ben when he's old enough to watch horror movies."

"They'll probably stick him in a virtual-reality machine, and if he doesn't run fast enough in his mind, he'll get ripped apart by some shiny, metallic techno-creature."

Veda laughed and turned her attention back to the screen. "That girl there, not the blond one, the one who's climbing down the side of the building, she has to be the worst actor I've ever seen, but you should hear her scream. She has a scream that could stop a freight train." She glanced back at Kate. "Are you going to watch the rest of it with me?"

Kate felt the restlessness twitch through her again, making it difficult to stand still. She pushed a rough hand through her hair and turned around. "No thanks. I'm going to get a glass of milk and go on up to bed."

Veda didn't hear her. The older woman was already talking to the girl on the screen, critiquing her performance, telling her how stupid she was to have gotten into the situation in the first place.

A few minutes later when Kate walked into her bedroom, she didn't turn on the lamp. She changed into a gown of pale blue satin, then went to the white rocking chair by the window and sat down.

While she drank her milk, she rocked. It wasn't a gentle, soothing motion. It was agitated and energetic, an outward expression of inner disquiet.

It was McKinsey Smith. Mac was causing these unfamiliar fidgety moods. Or, to be more precise, it was her feelings for Mac that were responsible.

That day at the hospital, she had been startled

by the suspicion that she could possibly be falling in love with him. But at the same time it had been only that, a slightly shocking, still-unconfirmed suspicion.

Now, after having lain awake for most of the past three, interminably long nights, after thinking back over every encounter since the day he had first turned up in her backyard, she knew the truth.

Kate wasn't falling in love with Mac. She had already fallen. Hard.

She exhaled a soft sigh. What good did it do her to admit it? There was certainly no one around to celebrate or bemoan her new state of heart.

Since the day of Ben's accident, Mac had taken great care to stay out of her way. And when they accidentally ran into each other, he avoided her eyes and made an excuse to leave as quickly as possible.

Even with Ben and Veda, he was different. He had suddenly, perceptibly withdrawn, pulling back into his shell, once again putting up the barriers that separated him from the rest of the world.

Kate rose to her feet and moved closer to the window. The lights were on in the garage apartment. Was he having trouble sleeping? Was he reliving the events that had caused the scars on his arms?

When she thought about the things he had told her in the hospital, when she thought about what he had lost and what he had endured, the images hurt her. But it was a strange kind of hurt. Personal. Intimate.

Now, as she stared at the lights in his windows, she couldn't bear the thought of his being alone over there as he tried to deal with the demons from his past.

Kate could help him. She was positive she could. If he would only let her.

What was it about men that made them think they had to handle the difficult things alone? Would it be showing some kind of unacceptable weakness if they occasionally admitted to needing the warmth and comfort of another human being?

A moment later, without giving herself a chance to have second thoughts, Kate abruptly pulled on the short robe that matched her gown and walked out of the bedroom. She didn't stop until she stood at the top of the wooden stairs.

Mac, bare from the waist up, opened the door at her knock. For a moment he simply stood staring down at her.

"Just a second and let me get a shirt," he said finally, and moved as if to close the door.

Reaching out, Kate put her hand against the door. "You don't need to do that. I'll only stay a minute. I just wanted to—"

When he moved slightly away from her, unwittingly allowing her to see one small part of his back, her breath caught sharply in her throat.

Turning his head, he watched her, his eyes narrowed and wary. Taking a step back, he shoved his hands into the pockets of his jeans.

"My God," Kate whispered as she came closer. Ignoring the way he stiffened, she moved behind him. "Oh Mac . . . your back. Your poor, poor back."

Raising one hand, she ran her fingers across the hard muscles scored with disfiguring scars. Then leaning forward, she pressed her lips to one deep scar near his left shoulder, only vaguely aware of his rasping groan of protest and the deep shudder that shook through his body.

Moving abruptly, he stepped away from her and walked to the bar, where he picked up a glass and swallowed the rest of its contents.

"What's the matter, Katie?" His voice was as stiff as his shoulders and he spoke without meeting her eyes. "Isn't there anyone around for you to play push-me, pull-you with? Are you afraid you'll get out of practice?"

Kate's head jerked back sharply in reflexive reaction to the harsh words, but she drew in a slow breath and forced herself to remain calm. Whether he liked it or not, she knew him now. And she understood why he felt he had to do this. It was a form of self-protection.

When she made no response, he continued his tirade. "As soon as I set eyes on the first of your men—I think it was Allbright—I knew then that I didn't have a thing in common with them. Other than Junior, they were all the Big Business don't-get-in-my-way-because-I'm-moving-too-fast-to-stop types.I didn't understand them, didn't really like them, but I damned sure pitied them. You had every single one of them fooled."

He glanced at her, then looked quickly away again. "Like an iceberg." His low whisper was distracted now, as though he were talking to himself rather than her. "Deep as hell and cold to the core."

Visibly shaking off the mood, he gave a rough laugh. "They just kept hanging around, letting you use them like trained chimps, hoping the day would come when you would feel something, hoping that someday you might actually need one of them. But they didn't know anything about you, did they? Kate the Mighty is a whole new model. A third sex. All-inclusive, sufficient unto yourself. If you ever find a way to reproduce yourself, you'll be a genuine threat to society."

Although Kate knew he was striking out at her from his own pain, using wild exaggeration to hurt her because he was hurting, the bitterness in his voice took her by surprise. And something about the grim lines around his mouth told her he wasn't pulling his accusations out of thin air. He actually believed that some of them were the truth.

"You're wrong." Frowning, she added, "At least, partly wrong. Maybe Julian and Gardner— Maybe it's like you said and they were waiting around, thinking I would eventually feel something for them. But how can you of all people accuse me of being cold? You know . . . you *know* I feel all the things a normal woman feels."

For an instant their eyes met and the memory of what had happened in the backyard was like a solid presence between them. A moment later his eyes changed and she saw him coldly, deliberately reject the shared memory.

When he walked to the window, turning his back on her, Kate cleared her throat and went on. "After David died, after I worked through the grief, I knew I had to start . . . to start living again. I tried— Mac, I *really* tried to feel something for the men I met." She moved closer as she gave the halting explanation. "But time after time I failed. That actually scared me a little. I thought something inside me was permanently damaged. But then I finally understood. I finally recognized what was going on. There was a reason I couldn't feel anything for those men. You see—" Breaking off, she shook her head. "It doesn't make sense and maybe you won't understand how—"

When she didn't continue immediately, he glanced over his shoulder. "Keep going. The reason you couldn't feel anything . . ."

Kate drew in a slow, steadying breath. "I finally realized that I couldn't begin a new love affair for the simple reason that I had never finished with the old." Her lips curved in a bemused smile. "Crazy, isn't it? After all these years, I was still connected to my husband. I was still waiting for David to come home."

Before she could even begin to explain that Mac had changed everything, he swung around to face her. Grabbing her by the shoulders, he almost lifted her off the ground as he gave her a good, hard shake.

"Don't you get it?" His face was close to hers, his golden eyes blazing with anger. "He isn't coming home. *David isn't ever coming back!*"

Kate didn't bother struggling, and she made no response to the ruthlessly shouted words. She simply stared into his eyes.

"I just had the craziest thought," she said, her voice low as her gaze wandered over his stiff features. "For a minute there, you almost sounded jealous."

A rough laugh caught in his throat. "Maybe I am. And you're right. It's crazy as hell." Releasing her, he shook his head and took a step back. "It's time for you to leave."

When she didn't move, his jaw tightened. "I'm warning you, Kate, you're playing around with something that's right out of your league."

And still she didn't leave.

Mac's golden eyes caught fire. There was anger in their depths, but that wasn't all. Satisfaction was there as well. Satisfaction and blatant, blazing desire. It was as though, even as he was mentally and physically pushing her away, this was what he secretly wanted.

"You've had your warning." A harsh laugh came from low in his throat as he turned and backed her against the wall, his gaze drifting down her body. "Now you have to take the consequences. It's Lady Chatterley time, Katie. Is that what turns you on, going to the gamekeeper's lodge for a little rough and ready sex?" He laughed again. "Those poor saps you've been dating didn't have a chance with you. They were the wrong class, weren't they, too refined to fulfill my lady's fantasies? I can't picture any of them getting down and dirty. They only know how to ... how to ..."

The words drifted off. He was staring at her mouth. "That little quiver in your lower lip fascinates the hell out of me." His voice was softer now, huskier. "It's strange how little things become important. Like a kiss." The last word whispered across her brow, stirring the fine hair at her temples. "You could get naked and screw until dawn and it could still be as impersonal as a handshake. But a kiss is different."

As he spoke he kept his gaze on her mouth,

making her lips throb and burn. "A kiss, full on the mouth, is personal. It's intimate. That night in the backyard, things got hot. Real hot. Through my shirt, I could feel your nipples getting tight. I could feel your heat on my thigh. I damn near felt the blood pulsing in your secret places. But I didn't kiss you. Not even to brush my mouth across yours. I knew you wouldn't have stopped me, and still I didn't let it happen. Because I didn't want things between us to get personal." He gave a soft, self-mocking laugh. "But you know what? When you deny yourself something you really want, even something as simple as a kiss, you find out that you can't stop thinking about it. You ache to have it, Katie. In your mind, it becomes more erotic, more seductive, than the act itself."

Reaching up, he pushed his fingers through the hair on either side of her face and, clasping her head, tilted it up. Then he slowly lowered his head. By the time she felt his warm breath on her lips, anticipation and desire had spread through every inch of her body, setting her on fire.

The first touch of his mouth brought a swift intake of breath, a sound that seemed to affect him enormously. With a low growl he began to devour her, moving her head first one way then the other to get more of her mouth.

The heat of his desire was a potent aphrodisiac, and the sheer force of it moved her, pulling at her, making her press more urgently against him. Only now, when he was finally holding her, finally kissing her and touching her, did she understand how long she had been wanting this to happen—maybe from the first moment she saw him—and how desperately and thoroughly she had wanted it to happen.

His hands slid down her back, settling on her hips, and he began bunching up the blue satin of her nightgown until only the sheer silk of her panties was between his clasping fingers and the flesh of her buttocks. Raising her, he fitted her against him, moving her hips up and down, letting his hardness stroke the warm, moist ache between her thighs.

When a moan escaped her, he eased slightly away so that her upper body rested against the wall, her hips were still pressed close to him, and the line of their bodies made a narrow V. Supporting her with one hand, he reached down into the small space between them and used the knuckle of one finger to caress the throbbing, sensitive mound, teasing and inciting, driving her wild with need.

Through half-closed eyes she saw his face, his tugged features tight and intense, his whiskey-colored eyes on fire with reckless hunger.

She blinked, then blinked again, trying to clear her vision. But it was no use. The room was fading. The world and hard reality were fading. There was only sensation.

His lips covered hers again, smothering her help-less whimper of pleasure. She dug her fingers into the hard muscle of his shoulders, sucking urgently at his tongue and lower lip.

Kate was begging, and she made no pretense that it was anything else. She didn't care anymore. She would beg, she would plead, she would bribe if she had to. She only knew she wanted more. Sweet heaven, she wanted it all.

When he groaned in response, the sound was low and rough. Lifting her into his arms, he carried her into the bedroom where they fell together onto the bed and began tearing at the other's clothing with frantic fingers.

A moment later, when he entered her, his first hard thrust was the most powerful thing she had ever felt and she cried out with the sweetness of it. Each sliding stroke, each hungry touch was spontaneous. Their bodies had taken over the wild coupling, their combined desire compelling their movements, urging them on to completion.

And when the climax came, it raged through them both in a breath-stealing, heart-shaking explosion of joy.

Kate was lying on her back, her head resting on Mac's shoulder, when she felt his touch on her face.

"You're crying," he said softly.

She moved her face against his shoulder, an unspoken gesture of gratitude. "It's the most amazing thing. I feel lighter. As though all the heavy things, pain and loneliness and self-doubt, had simply drained out of me. It's all gone."

She feathered a kiss across his bare chest. "I wish you could know what I'm feeling. It's like being resigned to the hopelessness of slavery, then suddenly, unexpectedly being set free." She moved her lips to his throat and again kissed the warm flesh. "Always before, when someone simply kissed me, it felt all wrong. It was like . . . like I was somehow betraying David."

She moved her head to stare up at the ceiling. "But with you, it's different."

She thought of David then and the way it used to be. But even as her husband's dear face flashed across her mind, Kate felt no guilt. What had happened between her and Mac still felt right.

David, her darling David, had always treated her gently, as though she were a fragile piece of china. But back then she had been fragile. Kate was a grown woman now. And apparently, as she changed, her needs changed as well.

"It felt so *right*," she whispered. "So wonderfully, beautifully right. It was the most incredibly exciting thing that's ever happened to me." She turned her head toward him, studying his face. "It was right for you, too, wasn't it? I mean, it wasn't just me?"

He gave a husky laugh, pulling her closer. "No, I was there with you. Every step of the way."

She exhaled a soft breath, warmed by the honest emotion in his voice. She hugged his arm tightly to her breast and began to run her fingers lightly across the scars as she studied his features.

"I can't imagine how you survived," she murmured. "You must have suffered terribly."

"I had a way of blocking out what was happening." He smiled. "It frustrated them, the way I could leave reality behind and go to a different place. A beautiful, gentle place where no hatred existed. There was only love and peace."

The words brought quick, hot tears to Kate's eyes. Although the tears were for his pain, they also contained an element of gladness. He was no longer shutting her out. There were no walls between them now. Mac was finally letting her see who he really was, an action that was, in its own way, as intimate as making love had been.

Her gaze drifted again over his features. "Sometimes . . . sometimes there's a look in your eyes that hurts me to see. Is that when you're remembering?"

"I have flashbacks," he said slowly, as though the words didn't come easily. "They come at me out of nowhere and I have to fight the need to run.

It's not as bad as it was in the beginning. I still have dreams once or twice a week that have me waking up in a cold sweat. When it happens, the reality of where I am can't reach me. In my mind, I'm back there, waiting for them to come in, waiting for it to start all over again."

Turning in his arms, she moved her head to smooth a kiss along his jaw. "Maybe . . . maybe if you had someone beside you when you wake up like that, she could hold onto you and keep you in the here and now." She glanced up at him from beneath her lashes. "You think?"

His only response was another husky laugh.

"What?" she asked, smiling with him, sharing his amused pleasure without knowing the cause.

"If I didn't know better, I'd say the Car-Wash Queen was propositioning me."

She made a soft sound of derision. "Well, apparently you don't know anything because that's exactly what I was doing."

Before the last word was out of her mouth, he was rolling over to cover her body with his.

David sat on a stool at the bar. It was three in the morning. Kate was asleep in the bedroom.

Spread out over the counter were the newspaper clippings he had gotten months earlier from the library. He pushed a pile of them aside and began to go through the material he had passed over before, the articles about his kidnapping and the months that followed.

After arranging them by date, he picked up the top one, an article from one of the local newspapers. Published two days after revolution broke out in Gamarra, it was a sketchy account of the kidnapping of David and his colleagues. As well as small pictures of the eight men involved, there was a larger picture of Kate. She looked pale, slightly dazed, and her enormous green eyes held terror as she shrank from reporters.

The following articles explored in detail what she went through in dealing with his abduction and how she fought to have him freed. The photographs that appeared with the articles were a record of change and after a year, a new maturity showed in her features. She stood with her shoulders back and her head high. There was inner strength in the way she now faced the cameras. This was a woman to be reckoned with. In these handful of photographs, David saw her grow up and get strong.

She had to get strong. She was taking on the world as she fought to have her husband freed. She bullied the press. She tackled the federal government. She talked to anyone who would listen to her. At first her words were soft and pleading, but that soon changed. Before long she was demanding that they listen to her, demanding that someone somewhere do something to have her husband released.

Finally David came to the last article in the pile and the accompanying photograph. The picture, taken on the day she had received the news of his death, was painful for him to see. She looked as dead as he was supposed to have been.

He knew without being told that Kathy died that day.

And Kate arose from the ashes, stronger and more resplendent. And she carried on. She began to make a new life for herself and her son.

Sliding off the stool, David walked slowly back to the bedroom. For a long time he stood beside the bed, staring down at her.

She had been through hell, as surely as he had.

But for her, the hell was over. She had a new life. A good life. The ugliness that still followed him, that still had the power to make him break out in a cold sweat, was not a part of her life.

She thought she could help him. She was a strong woman, but she didn't know what she would have to deal with. She couldn't imagine the things that had been done to him during captivity, the atrocities that were committed on a daily basis.

Leaning down, he gently brushed a lock of hair from her cheek, then let his hand linger on the soft, warm flesh.

She was an amazing woman, and she had fought

hard to become who she was. She deserved happiness. She deserved those nice, normal, permanent-press men. Men with no scars on their bodies, no scars on their souls.

Drawing in a slow breath, David forced himself to acknowledge the truth he had been holding back for days. He loved her. This strong, independent woman. This Kate. He loved her more than he loved life, more than he loved freedom.

And he knew the best gift he could ever give her was to leave her world.

ELEVEN

Opening her eyes slowly, Kate stared at the streaks of sunlight on the ceiling. As bits and pieces of the night before began to come back to her, she smiled. Falling asleep in Mac's bed. Hearing him speak softly to her as he wrapped her in a blanket. The sound of his footsteps on the stairs as he carried her up to her bedroom. Her sleepy protests when he left her.

She spread her arms, stretching slowly, luxuriously, reveling in the changes in her body. But her body wasn't the only thing that had changed. Today, the whole world was different. The sun was brighter. The air smelled sweeter. It was a brand new day, a day fairly bursting with promise.

She sat up and wrapped her arms around her bare knees. Only now did she realize how much she had missed this. The delicious feeling of anticipation. The suspicion that wonderment might be out there, just waiting for her to find it. For six years those feelings had been absent.

She gave a soft laugh when she remembered the way she had propositioned Mac the night before. He thought she was hinting for him to make love to her again. Kate had wanted that. Oh yes, she had definitely wanted that.

But that wasn't all she wanted. She wanted Mac in her life permanently. Not just for herself, although heaven knew she and Ben needed him. She wanted it for Mac as well. They would be good for him. She was sure of it. They could be there for him as he fought his way through the memory of hell. They would help him get his life back on track so that he wouldn't have to hide out anymore.

Jumping out of bed, she went into the bathroom and turned on the shower. As she pinned up her hair she paused for a moment, wondering what Mac's life had been like back before he lost his family, back before he ran into the people who hurt him.

Did those things happen simultaneously? Were they unrelated or separate steps in the same overall tragedy?

Whatever happened, however it happened, Kate couldn't understand how his ex-wife could have let him go. If Kate had been Mac's wife, she would have fought the devil himself to keep him.

There was so much she didn't know about him,

she acknowledged with a frown as she stepped into the shower. In fact, all she really knew for sure was that she loved him.

For now, that was enough. More than enough, much more than she had ever expected to find.

That Kate had no hesitation in admitting the way she felt about Mac surprised her a little. She had always believed that if she fell in love again, she would have to say good-bye to her husband, but it wasn't that way at all. David was still in her heart just as he had always been, just as he always would be. And somehow she knew he would have liked Mac.

No, she corrected silently, "like" was too tame a word. McKinsey Smith wasn't the sort of man to incite bland emotions. David would have been fascinated, as Kate was, by the twists and turns of Mac's mind.

Leaning her head back against the damp tile, she drew in a long, slow breath, warmed by the knowledge that David would have been happy for her. He had always wanted the best for her and Ben. And Mac was the best.

Suddenly Kate found herself laughing aloud from pure joy. She wanted to go outside and run in the sunshine. She wanted to hug a total stranger. She wanted to share what she felt with the world.

Minutes later, when she walked into the kitchen and found her housekeeper loading the dishwasher,

Kate walked across the room, wrapped her arms around Veda, and gave her an enthusiastic hug.

"Thank you for being here," Kate said with a quiver of laughter in her voice. "I had an uncontrollable urge to hug a stranger and I couldn't possibly find anyone stranger than my dear, dear Veda."

Pulling free, the older woman backed away and studied Kate with wary, narrowed eyes. "What in hell— Oh my God, it really happened, didn't it? Did you leave after I went to bed? Who— Oh no . . . no . . . no. I'm warning you, Kate, if you tell me you slept with Junior Thibideaux, you'd better get out of the way because I will probably throw up."

Kate laughed. "Don't be silly. Junior could never in a million years make me feel like this. It was someone you approve of, someone who fits into your 'real man' category." She smiled. "And someone much closer to home."

"Close to— *Mac*?" Veda drew back her head, one brow raised in speculation. "I was pretty sure something was happening between the two of you, but I could never tell if you were going to kill each other or jump into the nearest bed."

Kate laughed. "Luckily for me, it turned out to be the latter."

"My, my, aren't we smug about it. For the three years I've been here, you've been the Iron Maiden. Am I seeing the real you for the first time?"

"Maybe." Picking up a piece of bacon from a

plate on the stove, Kate took a bite, then glanced at the older woman. "So how do you like the real me?"

"If you get any more cute and perky, I may have to smack you." Veda shook her head and laughed. "I guess I could get used to it."

"If everything works out, you'll have to," Kate told her as she moved toward the backdoor. "Keep your fingers crossed."

Letting the screen slam behind her, she ran across the yard and up the wooden stairs to the garage apartment. When Mac opened the door to her knock, she practically threw herself into his arms.

"Good morning . . . good morning . . . good morning," she said, punctuating each greeting with a kiss.

For an instant, his arms tightened around her, then he pulled free and took a step back. "I'm glad you're here. I wanted to talk to you." His voice was distracted and he avoided looking directly at her. "Last night—"

"Last night was the most wonderful—"

"*Kate.*"

Something in his voice made her stop and stare at him. When her brow creased in concern, he swore under his breath.

"Last night should never have happened," he said abruptly, his voice tight. "It was a mistake. You took me by surprise and I— For Pete's sake, don't look at me like that. It's not like we took a vow or anything. You had a one night stand with your *handyman*. Time out for a reality check, lady."

Turning his back on her, he moved a few steps away, and when he spoke again, his voice was more gentle, more controlled. "That's all it can be, Kate. A fling. A temporary aberration. Getting involved . . . the two of us—" He broke off and shook his head in a helpless gesture. "It simply wouldn't work. It's not what I want, and when you've had time to think, you'll know it's not really what you want either."

Kate could only stand and stare at his stiff back, one hand held to her chest. With tightly clenched fingers, she was trying to contain the sharp, breath-stealing pain that had settled there, trying to hold it in, to keep it from growing.

When her heart finally stopped its frantic pounding, when she was finally able to draw in a normal breath, her brain began to work again. And that was when she knew: Mac was lying.

Raising her chin, she studied his face. So he wasn't going to make it easy. She should have expected it.

Last night he had let her get too close, he had let her see too much. For just a little while he had stopped playing the tough guy and had let her see that he was vulnerable. For a man as strong as Mac, as wary as Mac, that must have been a scary thing. So now he was trying desperately to take a step backward. For his own protection, he was trying to put patches on the holes in his armor.

The silence between them drew out and after a moment he cleared his throat. "I'm sorry if I seemed blunt, but I figured it would be better, more honest, to tell you how I feel now, before any real damage is done."

When she didn't respond, he shoved his hands in his back pockets and glanced away from her. "I'd better get to work now. I promised Ben we would finish the treehouse this afternoon and there are some things I need to take care of first."

"Sure." She drew in an unsteady breath and turned toward the door. "You go ahead. We can talk later."

"Kate—" When she glanced back at him, he met her gaze for a moment, studying her expression with narrowed eyes, then he simply shook his head. "Never mind. Like you said, we can talk later."

Kate returned to the house and walked through the kitchen without looking at Veda. She went up the stairs and into her bedroom.

For most of the morning, she simply stood at the window and watched him. Later in the day, after Ben came home from Chad's, she watched the two of them as they put finishing touches on the treehouse.

Before she had even left the garage apartment, Kate had turned everything off. Thoughts, emotions, everything was put on hold. She knew she would drive herself crazy if she let herself remember his tone, his words, the wall he had intentionally put between them. Until she regained some objectivity, she couldn't think about it. So she simply watched and waited.

The sun was low in the west when Kate moved away from the window. Mac and Ben were through with the treehouse. Later was finally here.

As she walked down the stairs her steps slowed as doubt began to nudge her.

What if she was wrong? What if it really was all on her side? Was she simply fooling herself into believing that Mac loved her, that he needed her as much as she needed him?

A fling? A one-night stand? Was that really all it had been for him?

Walking out the front door, she went around the house to the garage so that neither Ben nor Mac would see her. She would wait for him in the apartment.

And one way or another, she would find the truth. No matter what it was, no matter how it hurt, she wanted the truth now.

Inside the apartment, Kate walked to the window that looked down on the backyard. Mac and Ben were still together, standing in the shade of the oak tree as they talked. Or rather, as Mac talked. From where she stood, his voice was faint but audible.

"We'll still be friends, Ben. Best buddies, remember. We'll talk every day on the telephone . . . and we'll still do things together. You understand that, don't you, son? Just because I won't live here anymore doesn't mean we can't still be friends."

Kate pressed closer to the window, frowning. What was he saying? Why was he talking about leaving?

"But, Mac—"

"This is the way it has to be." He paused, his voice low and rough. "Things don't always work out the way you want them to. You have to adjust, make compromises. When life changes, you have to change with it."

And then, as Kate watched, he reached up and cleared the leaves out of the knothole in the oak tree.

Kate frowned in confusion. How had he found it? Not even Ben, who had explored every inch of the backyard, knew the knothole was there.

A moment later, Mac pulled something from the knothole and, with his head bent, stood looking at it for a long time.

"What's that?" Ben asked. "What are you doing, Mac?"

"I'm just taking care of a loose end." He raised his head slightly. "Let it be a lesson for you, son. Forever doesn't last as long as you think."

Kate couldn't move. She couldn't think. She couldn't catch her breath. Then a moment later everything started again in a frantic rush. As she sucked in a breath of air, her body began to shake and she was dizzy with the wildness of her thoughts.

When her legs threatened to give way, she swung around and leaned back against the wall beside the window.

How did he know? Was he psychic? Had he somehow looked into her past and seen the night that she and David had gone into the backyard and—

Giving her head a violent shake, she pulled herself upright and began to move toward the door.

It was crazy, she told herself as she left the apartment. The whole thing was preposterous. Insane.

She had no idea where she was going as she ran down the stairs and away from the garage. She only knew she had to think. She had to try to—

David's eyes.

Kate stopped in her tracks, one hand pressed to her mouth, her eyes wide in shock. Sweet heaven, Mac had David's eyes! They were the same color. They darkened when he made love. They grew lighter when he laughed. *David's eyes.*

She had to stop thinking like that. She had to be reasonable. Mac's eyes might be the same color as David's, but that meant nothing. His eyes were similar. His hair was the same color and texture as David's. But Mac's face and husky-whisper voice were different. They were *different*.

But then her steps began to slow again. What had Mac told her about being tortured?

I wandered onto their turf. . . . Some people are very territorial.

Was his throat injured at the same time he got the scars? Had his face been injured as well?

The wrong place at the wrong time.

Gamarra?

Closing her eyes tightly, Kate forced herself to remember those terrible photographs, the ones that had proved her husband was dead. David's face had been destroyed. Not a single feature had been left intact. Only by the process of elimination had he been identified.

A different face. A different voice.

No, she told herself, shaking her head in vehement denial. *No!* What she was thinking was insane. There had to be another explanation.

But Mac *knew* things, she argued silently. He had known about her liberal arts degree and that she had once been a painter. From the very beginning, he had known his way around the house. He knew where things were located without being told, and his only explanation had been that he was using logical deduction.

Suddenly her breath caught in a hoarse gasp. *That dream*. In her dream, David and Mac had somehow become one person. And later, when they had finally made love, it had felt right. Dear God in heaven, it had felt so right.

Pressing her hands to her flushed cheeks, she moistened her trembling lips. She had just remembered something else. McKinsey was David's mother's maiden name.

There were too many things. *Too many*. There was no way it could all be a bizarre set of coincidences. There were simply too many things.

A moment later, when Kate heard a car pull up beside her, she realized she was standing on the sidewalk in front of the house, both hands clasped to her chest.

Glancing around, she saw Ralph get out of his car and walk around the front.

"I can only stay a minute," he said as he moved toward her. "I just thought I'd stop by and see if Ben wanted to—" He broke off and stared at her. "What's wrong? What happened?"

She took an awkward step toward him. "Who is he, Ralph? You know. You sent him here." Reaching out, she grasped his hand with shaking fingers. "You have to tell me the truth. *Who is he?*"

The older man's face was flushed, his movements agitated. "What are you— Listen, you have to understand—" He swallowed heavily, then drew in a slow breath. "Dammit, Kate, I can't say anything. I don't have the right."

"You don't have to," she whispered, shaking her head slowly. "I know."

Turning around, she began to walk toward the backyard.

"Kate . . . Kate, *wait*!"

She ignored the urgency in Ralph's voice and kept walking. When she reached the backyard, when she stood in the shade of the oak, she glanced down at her son. "Go inside with Veda, Ben."

"Make Mac stay, Mom." Tears were shining in Ben's brown eyes and his voice trembled. "Tell him he can't go away from us. Tell him we *need* him."

"We'll talk about it later. Right now I want you to go inside."

As Ben walked away, the man beside the tree kept his gaze on her face, his eyes narrowed, as though he were trying to read what was behind her stony expression.

After a moment, Kate shook her head unsteadily. She couldn't bring herself to say the words. Even though she knew the truth, she couldn't bring herself to say the words.

"Was it some kind of game?" she finally managed to ask.

He swallowed heavily, then turned his head slightly to the side, his expression wary. "I don't know what you're talking about."

"What's in your hand?" she asked.

When his fingers clenched around the cork, the movement automatic and defensive, Kate swallowed a whimper and closed her eyes.

"How could you?" she asked in a hoarse whisper. "I don't understand. I just don't understand why you did this to me."

Opening her eyes, she moved a step closer. "Just say it," she demanded, her voice shaking with anger. "Go on and say it. Say, 'I'm David. I'm your husband come back from the dead.' Damn you, *say it*!"

"I'm David," he whispered.

Kate brought both hands up to cover her face as a violent shudder ripped through her body. A moment later, she turned around and walked away. She felt his hand on her shoulder almost immediately.

"Kate . . . Kate, please," he begged. "Let me explain."

With a violent gesture, she shrugged off his hand and moved several steps away from him. She couldn't do anything—she couldn't *think*—until she put some space between them. She had to decide what to do. She had to figure out what to say.

"Did you come back to check me out and see if you still wanted me for your wife?" Her voice shook and she spoke without turning around. "If I failed the test, you could move on and let me go on believing you dead. If I passed, then what? Were you going to stay? As David or as Mac? Which was it going to be, the old love or the new?"

Tilting her head back, she gave a short, angry laugh. "But I didn't pass the test, did I? You're leaving. Was it something about last night? Couldn't you have made allowances for the fact that I'm a little out of practice in the sex department? If you give me some time, I'm sure I could do better."

"*Let . . . me . . . explain,*" he said again, the words low and slow and emphatic.

Keeping her head turned away from him, Kate waved a hand, indicating he was free to do as he chose.

When he finally began to speak, the words were rough with emotion. "I'm not going to give you details of those six years. I don't ever want you to know what they—" He broke off and a moment passed before he continued. "But I want you to know how I felt during the time I was gone. You need to know— I would like for you to know that the only thing that kept me alive was the thought of getting back to you and Ben."

Kate heard the intensity, the deep pain in his rough-whisper voice, and against her will, she found herself aching to take him in her arms. Glancing over her shoulder, she found that instead of moving closer, he had moved away from her.

He shoved his hands in his pockets and shrugged,

a tense, awkward movement of his shoulders. "Then I came back and found out you had both grown up without me. I wasn't necessary. You did it all without me." His lips twisted in a self-mocking smile. "That hurt. You couldn't believe how much it hurt. I needed you both so desperately, but there you were doing just fine without me. Better than fine."

This time his smile contained genuine, if rueful amusement. "I actually thought I hated you. I felt like this beautiful, sophisticated woman had— I know this sounds crazy, but it felt as though you had killed the woman I left behind. I wanted to make you pay. For growing, for changing, for not needing me. I took every chance I got to torment you." He met her eyes. "I'm sorry to say, I even thought about trying to take Ben away from you. But then I got to know you."

Shaking his head, he gave a rough laugh. "That left me more confused than ever. Against my will I found myself wanting you. Even worse, I found myself liking you. Then last night— Well, you know what happened last night. You walked in and gave me the chance to do what I had been aching to do since the day you interviewed me." His voice dropped to a whisper, and his gaze roamed restlessly over her body. "I didn't intend for it to happen, but there was no way I could stop it."

He paused, drawing in a slow, ragged breath. "Later, while you were sleeping in my bed, I knew it was time for me to face up to a few things, so I pulled out some old newspaper clippings. I read them all. I found out what you went through when I was taken hostage, and later when you believed I was dead. I already knew why I changed, and last night I finally understood why you had. Same reason for both of us. We each did what we had to do to survive."

He moved his shoulders, as though they were tender. "I came back here needing to be needed. If you had been the same as when I left—inexperienced, shy, and vulnerable—I could have taken charge. I could have thrown myself into the job of taking care of you and Ben." He rubbed his jaw with stiff fingers. "After so many years of having control taken away from me, of not being allowed even the smallest amount of personal freedom, I would finally be the one in control. I thought that would make everything right again. I would feel like a man instead of a whipped animal."

Raising his head, he met her eyes. "You were right when you said I was still carrying the past around. And it's nightmare stuff, Kate. I'm not talking about what they did to my body. The worst part is what they did to my mind. There are things I won't be able to talk about for a long time, maybe never."

He shook his head. "You fought hard to get where you are now, and I can't tell you how proud

I am of you, of the success you've achieved. But my fight isn't finished. It wouldn't be fair to you to—" He broke off and took a step toward her. "Don't you see? *You deserve something better than what I've become.* The scars aren't only on my arms and back. I'm scarred inside as well. Katie, I came back here with a different face, a different voice, and a different soul." The muscle beside his mouth twitched violently. "You should have someone who isn't carrying around a lot of freaking trash from the past."

All the anger had drained out of her as though it had never existed. Nothing she felt, none of the doubts or fears, could come close to what he had been through.

But now it was time to heal. She had to make him understand. She had to make him see the truth.

"I don't need you?" The words came out thin with emotion. "Is that what you said? Didn't you hear anything I said to you last night? For heaven's sake, think about it."

She drew in a slow bracing breath. "Remember when you told me I was going backward emotionally? Well, you were right about that, and I told you . . . last night I tried to explain the reason behind it. At first it was from shock. But later it was intentional. When I felt myself beginning to return to normal emotionally, I fought against it. I backed away from it. Because it would be like building a house when there was no one to live in it. If David— If you weren't here, if the man I love wasn't ever coming back to me, I simply didn't want to be whole."

She took a step forward, closing the distance between them. "I've met a lot of men in the past six years. Good men. Attractive men. Men who were sexy as hell and had their heads on straight to boot. But not a single one of them reached me. Not one of them reached me in here," she said, laying a hand against her breasts.

She took another cautious step. "But then you turned up, and I couldn't stop the changes from happening. Don't you see? It was out of my hands. For you, I came alive again. Only for you."

When he simply stared at her, the pain still in his golden eyes, Kate began to get desperate. She wasn't reaching him. He was still holding himself separate. He was still keeping a wall between them.

Moistening her lips, she gestured back toward the house. "And what about Ben? You've been here only three months and already he depends on you more than people he's known all his life. He trusted you instinctively. He loves you, David."

When he still didn't respond, Kate gritted her teeth. She wouldn't give up. Damn him, she *would not give up*.

"I don't know what we would have been like if

things had gone the way we planned when we first got married," she said slowly. "I can look back and feel the sweetness of those days. It's a wonderful, soft feeling. Gentle and warm. Then I think of the way I love you now, the way you make me think about things, the way I feel when you hold me . . . as though it would kill you to let me go."

Drawing in a trembling breath, she said, "If it were possible, would I change you back to what you were six years ago? I would take away the pain you had to endure during those years. Dear God, I would give anything to make that go away. But I can't even think about giving you up, this man you are now. I couldn't do it."

She met his eyes. "Could you? You have our forever right there in your hand. Make a wish on it, David. Close your eyes and wish that I could somehow go back and be who I was back then."

Closing his eyes, he leaned his head back. "I can't," he said in a rough whisper. "I want *you*. I love *you*."

When he opened his eyes again, she saw the truth of his words there. But a moment later, he shook his head. "It doesn't matter. How I feel isn't the issue. I've known since the day of Ben's accident exactly how I feel about you. I love you so much it fills me up and makes it hard to breathe. If I let go, if I didn't hold it tight, my love for you would push everything else out of the way. But I can't let go. Don't you see? I love you enough to want something better than me for you."

"There *is* nothing better." Reaching out, she framed his face with her hands. "All the things you're worried about, what happened to you in Gamarra, all that is a part of you now. And I want it, David. I want every piece of you, the good and the bad. Last night when I came to you, I knew about the ghosts that are haunting you, but that didn't stop me from proposing."

Her lips trembled in a tentative smile. "I told you I had learned how to fight. Well, I wasn't exaggerating. I would fight anyone or anything that tries to come between us. Even you."

Leaning forward, she pressed her lips against his. "I'm selfish," she murmured. "I want it all. I want the memory of what we were and the reality of what we've become."

A groan caught in his throat and a moment later he pulled her into his arms. His body shook as he held her tightly, the same way he had held her the night before, as though it would kill him to have to let her go.

"This is wrong," he whispered hoarsely. "*I'm* wrong. You need—"

"Why don't you let me decide what I need?" Framing his face with her hands, she looked into his eyes, his wonderful golden eyes. "Don't you see what's happened? We've been given a wonderful gift, David. Think about where most people are after eight years of marriage. They've settled into a routine, not quite sure of how they feel about each other anymore. But for us, a miracle happened. We were given the chance to fall in love all over again."

Smiling, she ran her thumb slowly over his lower lip and whispered, "Somebody up there likes us."

"Who? Who likes us?"

Ben was in the swing, leaning back as he looked up at them. "Who likes us?" he asked again.

" 'Us,' " David repeated, his voice rough with emotion as he placed one rough palm on Kate's cheek. "I'm still not sure this is going to work, but sweet Jesus, I like the sound of that."

Something was growing in his eyes. She could see it, and she could put a name to it. Hope.

Pulling his gaze away from her, David glanced down at his son. "What do you think, Ben? Do you think we feel kind of like a family?"

Turning around in the swing, the boy scrambled up on his knees, holding on to the ropes as he looked from Kate to David. "You mean you're going to stay? And you won't be the handyman anymore? You'll be my dad now?"

Kate glanced at David. The words needed to be said, for the man as well as for the boy. "He's always been your dad, Ben."

Ben cocked his small head to the side. "Huh?"

"You know those scars on my arms and back?" As he spoke, David kept his gaze on the boy's upturned face. "The thing is, I got hurt on my face too. And when they fixed me up, they made my face look different. I don't look like those pictures anymore, but I'm still me. I'm still David Moore. I'm your father, Ben."

"You mean you're my real dad and you didn't really get dead?" Rolling his eyes, he stood up on the swing to be taller. "Well, silly, why didn't you tell me that first?"

"Yeah, silly," Kate repeated. "Why didn't you tell us that first?"

David drew in a deep breath and, with a smile, shook his head. "I guess . . . I guess because I'm silly."

When Ben laughed, David handed him the cork. "Here, son, you can keep this as a souvenir. I don't need to hide forever in an old knothole."

Reaching out, David picked up Ben. With one arm around his son and the other around his wife, he held them both close.

"I've got my forever right here," he said, meeting Kate's eyes. "Right where it's supposed to be."

THE EDITOR'S CORNER

Celebrate the most romantic month of the year with LOVESWEPT! In the six fabulous novels coming your way, you'll thrill to the sexiest heroes and cheer for the most spirited heroines as they discover the power of passion. It's all guaranteed to get you in the mood for love.

Starting the lineup is the ever-popular Fayrene Preston with **STORM SONG**, LOVESWEPT #666—and Noah McKane certainly comes across like a force of nature. He's the hottest act in town, but he never gives interviews, never lets anyone get close to him—until Cate Gallin persuades the powerfully sensual singer to let her capture him on film. Nobody knows the secret they share, the bonds of pain and emotion that go soul-deep . . . or the risks they're taking when Cate accepts the challenge to reveal his stunning talent—without hurting the only man she's ever loved. This compelling novel is proof positive of why Fayrene is one of the best-loved authors of the genre.

SLIGHTLY SHADY by Jan Hudson, LOVE-SWEPT #667, is Maggie Marino's first impression of the brooding desperado she sees in the run-down bar. On the run from powerful forces, she's gotten stranded deep in the heart of Texas, and the last thing she wants is to tangle with a mesmerizing outlaw who calls himself Shade. But Shade knows just how to comfort a woman, and Maggie soon finds herself surrendering to his sizzling looks—even as she wonders what secret he's hiding. To tantalize you even further, we'll tell you that Shade is truly Paul Berringer, a tiger of the business world and brother of the Berringer twins who captivated you in **BIG AND BRIGHT** and **CALL ME SIN**. So don't miss out on Paul's own story. Bad boys don't come any better, and as usual Jan Hudson's writing shines with humor and sizzles with sensuality.

Please give a warm welcome to Gayle Kasper and her very first LOVESWEPT, **TENDER, LOVING CURE**, #668. As you may have guessed, this utterly delightful romance features a doctor, and there isn't a finer one than Joel Benedict. He'd do anything to become even better—except attend a sex talk seminar. He changes his mind, though, when he catches a glimpse of the teacher. Maggie Springer is a temptress who makes Joel think of private lessons, and when a taste of her kissable lips sparks the fire beneath his cool facade, he starts to believe that it's possible for him to love once more. We're happy to be Gayle's publisher, and this terrific novel will show you why.

Sally Goldenbaum returns to LOVESWEPT with **MOONLIGHT ON MONTEREY BAY**, #669. The beach in that part of California has always been special to Sam Eastland, and when he goes to his empty house there, he doesn't expect to discover a beautiful nymph. Interior decorator Maddie Ames fights to convince him that only she can create a sanctuary to soothe his troubled spirit . . . and he's too spellbound to refuse. But when their attraction flares into burning passion and Sam fears he can't give Maddie the joy she deserves, she must persuade him not to underestimate the power of love. Vibrant with heartfelt emotion, this romance showcases Sally's evocative writing. Welcome back, Sally!

A spooky manor house, things that go bump in the night—all this and more await you in **MIDNIGHT LADY**, LOVESWEPT #670, by Linda Wisdom. The granddaughter of the king of horror movies, Samantha Lyons knows all about scare tactics, and she uses them to try to keep Kyle Fletcher from getting the inside scoop about her family's film studio. But the devastatingly handsome reporter isn't about to abandon the story—or break the sensual magic that has woven itself around him and beautiful Sam . . . even if wooing her means facing down ghosts! Hold on to your seats because Linda is about to take you on a roller-coaster ride of dangerous desires and exquisite sensations.

It **LOOKS LIKE LOVE** when Drew Webster first sees Jill Stuart in Susan Connell's new LOVESWEPT, #671. Jill is a delicious early-morning surprise, clad in silky lingerie, kneeling in Drew's uncle's yard, and coaxing a puppy into her arms. Drew knows instantly that she wouldn't have to beg him to come running, and he sets off on a passionate courtship. To Jill, temptation has never looked or felt so good, but when Drew insists that there's a thief in the retirement community she manages, she tells him it can't be true, that she has everything under control. Drew wants to trust her, but can he believe the angel who's stolen his heart?

Susan delivers a wonderful love story that will warm your heart.

Happy reading!

With warmest wishes,

Nita Taublib

Nita Taublib

Associate Publisher

P.S. Don't miss the exciting women's novels from Bantam that are coming your way in February—**THE BELOVED SCOUNDREL** by nationally bestselling author Iris Johansen, a tempestuous tale of abduction, seduction, and surrender that sweeps from the shimmering halls of Regency England to the decadent haunts of a notorious rogue; **VIXEN** by award-winning author Jane Feather, a spectacular historical romance in which an iron-willed nobleman suddenly becomes the guardian of a mischievous, orphaned beauty; and **ONE FINE DAY** by supertalented Theresa Weir, which tells the searing story of a second chance for happiness for Molly and Austin Bennet, two memorable characters from Theresa's previous novel **FOREVER**. We'll be giving you a sneak peek at these terrific books in next month's LOVESWEPTs. And immediately following this page look for a preview of the exciting romances from Bantam that are *available now!*

Don't miss these exciting books by your
favorite Bantam authors

On sale in December:

DESIRE
by Amanda Quick

LONG TIME COMING
by Sandra Brown

STRANGER IN MY ARMS
by R.J. Kaiser

WHERE DOLPHINS GO
by Peggy Webb

And in hardcover from Doubleday
AMAZON LILY
by Theresa Weir

Amanda Quick

New York Times bestselling author of
DANGEROUS and **DECEPTION**

DESIRE

This spectacular novel is Amanda Quick's first medieval romance!

*From the windswept, craggy coast of a remote British isle comes
the thrilling tale of a daring lady and a dangerous knight who are
bound by the tempests of fate and by the dawning of desire . . .*

"There was something you wished to discuss with me, sir?"

"Aye. Our marriage."

Clare flinched, but she did not fall off the bench. Under
the circumstances, she considered that a great accomplish-
ment. "You are very direct about matters, sir."

He looked mildly surprised. "I see no point in being
otherwise."

"Nor do I. Very well, sir, let me be blunt. In spite of
your efforts to establish yourself in everyone's eyes as the
sole suitor for my hand, I must tell you again that your
expectations are unrealistic."

"Nay, madam," Gareth said very quietly. "'Tis your
expectations that are unrealistic. I read the letter you sent
to Lord Thurston. It is obvious you hope to marry a phantom, a man who does not exist. I fear you must settle for
something less than perfection."

She lifted her chin. "You think that no man can be found who suits my requirements?"

"I believe that we are both old enough and wise enough to know that marriage is a practical matter. It has nothing to do with the passions that the troubadours make so much of in their foolish ballads."

Clare clasped her hands together very tightly. "Kindly do not condescend to lecture me on the subject of marriage, sir. I am only too well aware that in my case it is a matter of duty, not desire. But in truth, when I composed my recipe for a husband, I did not believe that I was asking for so very much."

"Mayhap you will discover enough good points in me to satisfy you, madam."

Clare blinked. "Do you actually believe that?"

"I would ask you to examine closely what I have to offer. I think that I can meet a goodly portion of your requirements."

She surveyed him from head to toe. "You most definitely do not meet my requirements in the matter of size."

"Concerning my size, as I said earlier, there is little I can do about it, but I assure you I do not generally rely upon it to obtain my ends."

Clare gave a ladylike snort of disbelief.

"'Tis true. I prefer to use my wits rather than muscle whenever possible."

"Sir, I shall be frank. I want a man of peace for this isle. Desire has never known violence. I intend to keep things that way. I do not want a husband who thrives on the sport of war."

He looked down at her with an expression of surprise. "I have no love of violence or war."

Clare raised her brows. "Are you going to tell me that you have no interest in either? You, who carry a sword with a terrible name? You, who wear a reputation as a destroyer of murderers and thieves?"

"I did not say I had no interest in such matters. I have, after all, used a warrior's skills to make my way in the world. They are the tools of my trade, that's all."

"A fine point, sir."

"But a valid one. I have grown weary of violence, madam. I seek a quiet, peaceful life."

Clare did not bother to hide her skepticism. "An interesting statement, given your choice of career."

"I did not have much choice in the matter of my career," Gareth said. "Did you?"

"Nay, but that is—"

"Let us go on to your second requirement. You wrote that you desire a man of cheerful countenance and even temperament."

She stared at him, astonished. "You consider yourself a man of cheerful countenance?"

"Nay, I admit that I have been told my countenance is somewhat less than cheerful. But I am most definitely a man of even temperament."

"I do not believe that for a moment, sir."

"I promise you, it is the truth. You may inquire of anyone who knows me. Ask Sir Ulrich. He has been my companion for years. He will tell you that I am the most even-tempered of men. I am not given to fits of rage or foul temper."

Or to mirth and laughter, either, Clare thought as she met his smoky crystal eyes. "Very well, I shall grant that you may be even-tempered in a certain sense, although that was not quite what I had in mind."

"You see? We are making progress here." Gareth reached up to grasp a limb of the apple tree. "Now, then, to continue. Regarding your last requirement, I remind you yet again that I can read."

Clare cast about frantically for a fresh tactic. "Enough, sir. I grant that you meet a small number of my requirements if one interprets them very broadly. But what about our own? Surely there are some specific things you seek in a wife."

"My requirements?" Gareth looked taken back by the question. "My requirements in a wife are simple, madam. I believe that you will satisfy them."

"Because I hold lands and the recipes of a plump perfume business? Think twice before you decide that is sufficient to satisfy you sir. We live a simple life here on Desire. Quite boring in most respects. You are a man who is no doubt accustomed to the grand entertainments provided in the households of great lords."

"I can do without such entertainments, my lady. They hold no appeal for me."

"You have obviously lived an adventurous, exciting life," Clare persisted. "Will you find contentment in the business of growing flowers and making perfumes?"

"Aye, madam, I will," Gareth said with soft satisfaction.

"'Tis hardly a career suited to a knight of your reputation, sir."

"Rest assured that here on Desire I expect to find the things that are most important to me."

Clare lost patience with his reasonableness. "And just what are those things, sir?"

"Lands, a hall of my own, and a woman who can give me a family." Gareth reached down and pulled her to her feet as effortlessly as though she were fashioned of thistledown. "You can provide me with all of those things, lady. That makes you very valuable to me. Do not imagine that I will not protect you well. And do not think that I will let you slip out of my grasp."

"But—"

Gareth brought his mouth down on hers, silencing her protest.

LONG TIME COMING

by

SANDRA BROWN

Blockbuster author Sandra Brown—whose name is almost synonymous with the *New York Times* bestseller list—offers up a classic romantic novel that aches with emotion and sizzles with passion . . .

For sixteen years Marnie Hibbs had raised her sister's son as her own, hoping that her love would make up for the father David would never know . . . dreaming that someday David's father would find his way back into her life. And then one afternoon Marnie looked up and Law Kincaid was there, as strong and heartbreakingly handsome as ever. Flooded with bittersweet memories, Marnie yearned to lose herself in his arms, yet a desperate fear held her back, for this glorious man who had given her David now had the power to take him away. . . .

The Porsche crept along the street like a sleek black panther. Hugging the curb, its engine purred so deep and low it sounded like a predator's growl.

Marnie Hibbs was kneeling in the fertile soil of her flower bed, digging among the impatiens under the ligustrum bushes and cursing the little bugs that made three meals a day of them, when the sound of the car's motor attracted her attention. She glanced at it over her shoulder, then panicked as it came to a stop in front of her house.

"Lord, is it that late?" she muttered. Dropping her trowel, she stood up and brushed the clinging damp earth off her bare knees.

She reached up to push her dark bangs off her forehead before she realized that she still had on her heavy gardening gloves. Quickly she peeled them off and dropped them beside the trowel, all the while watching the driver get out of the sports car and start up her front walk.

Glancing at her wristwatch, she saw that she hadn't lost track of time. He was just very early for their appointment, and as a result, she wasn't going to make a very good first impression. Being hot, sweaty, and dirty was no way to meet a client. And she needed this commission badly.

Forcing a smile, she moved down the sidewalk to greet him, nervously trying to remember if she had left the house and studio reasonably neat when she decided to do an hour's worth of yard work. She had planned to tidy up before he arrived.

She might look like the devil, but she didn't want to appear intimidated. Self-confident friendliness was the only way to combat the disadvantage of having been caught looking her worst.

He was still several yards away from her when she greeted him. "Hello," she said with a bright smile. "Obviously we got our signals switched. I thought you weren't coming until later."

"I decided this diabolical game of yours had gone on long enough."

Marnie's sneakers skidded on the old concrete walk as she came to an abrupt halt. She tilted her head in stunned surprise. "I'm sorry, I—"

"Who the hell are you, lady?"

"Miss Hibbs. Who do you think?"

"Never heard of you. Just what the devil are you up to?"

"Up to?" She glanced around helplessly, as though the giant sycamores in her front yard might provide an answer to this bizarre interrogation.

"Why've you been sending me those letters?"

"Letters?"

He was clearly furious, and her lack of comprehension only seemed to make him angrier. He bore down on her like a hawk on a field mouse, until she had to bow her back to look up at him. The summer sun was behind him, casting him in silhouette.

He was blond, tall, trim, and dressed in casual slacks and a sport shirt—all stylish, impeccably so. He was wearing opaque aviator glasses, so she couldn't see his eyes, but if they were as belligerent as his expression and stance, she was better off not seeing them.

"I don't know what you're talking about."

"The letters, lady, the letters." He strained the words through a set of strong white teeth.

"*What* letters?"

"Don't play dumb."

"Are you sure you've got the right house?"

He took another step forward. "I've got the right house," he said in a voice that was little more than a snarl.

"Obviously you don't." She didn't like being put on the defensive, especially by someone she'd never met over something of which she was totally ignorant. "You're either crazy or drunk, but in any case, you're *wrong*. I'm not the person you're looking for and I demand that you leave my property. Now."

"You were expecting me. I could tell by the way you spoke to me."

"I thought you were the man from the advertising agency."

"Well, I'm not."

"Thank God." She would hate having to do business with someone this irrational and ill-tempered.

"You know damn well who I am," he said, peeling off the sunglasses.

Marnie sucked in a quick, sharp breath and fell back a step because she did indeed know who he was. She raised a hand to her chest in an attempt at keeping her jumping heart in place. "Law," she gasped.

"That's right. Law Kincaid. Just like you wrote it on the envelopes."

She was shocked to see him after all these years, standing only inches in front of her. This time he wasn't merely a familiar image in the newspaper or on her television screen. He was flesh and blood. The years had been kind to that flesh, improving his looks, not eroding them.

She wanted to stand and stare, but he was staring at her with unmitigated contempt and no recognition at all. "Let's go inside, Mr. Kincaid," she suggested softly.

STRANGER IN MY ARMS

by

R.J. KAISER

With the chilling tension of Hitchcock and the passionate heat of Sandra Brown, STRANGER IN MY ARMS is a riveting novel of romantic suspense in which a woman with amnesia suspects she is a target for murder.

Here is a look at this powerful novel . . .

"Tell me who you are, Carter, where you came from, about your past—everything."

He complied, giving me a modest summary of his life. He'd started his career in New York and formed a partnership with a British firm in London. When his partners suffered financial difficulties, he convinced my father to buy them out. Altogether he'd been in Europe for twelve years.

Carter was forty, ten years older than I. He'd been born and raised in Virginia, where his parents still resided. He'd attended Dartmouth and the Harvard Business School. In addition to the villa he had a house in Kensington, a flat off the avenue Bosquet in Paris, and a small farm outside Charlottesville, Virginia.

After completing his discourse, he leaned back and sipped his coffee. I watched him while Yvonne cleared the table.

Carter Bass was an attractive man with sophistication and class. He was well-spoken, educated. But mainly he appealed to me because I felt a connection with him, tortured though it was. We'd been dancing around each other since he'd appeared on the scene, our history at war with our more immediate and intangible feelings toward each other.

I could only assume that the allure he held for me had to do with the fact that he was both a stranger and my husband. My body, in effect, remembered Carter as my mind could not.

I picked up my coffee cup, but paused with it at my lips. Something had been troubling me for some time and I decided to blurt it out. "Do you have a mistress, Carter?"

He blinked. "What kind of a question is that?"

"A serious one. You know all about me, it's only fair I know about you."

"I don't have a mistress."

"Are you lonely?"

He smiled indulgently. "Hillary, we have an unspoken agreement. You don't ask and neither do I."

"Then you don't want to talk about it? I should mind my own business, is that what you mean?"

He contemplated me. "Maybe we should step out onto the terrace for some air—sort of clear our mental palate."

"If you like."

Carter came round and helped me up. "Could I interest you in a brandy?"

"I don't think so. I enjoyed the wine. That's really all I'd like."

He took my arm and we went through the salon and onto the terrace. He kept his hand on my elbow, though I was no longer shaky. His attention was flattering, and I decided I liked the changing chemistry between us, even though I had so many doubts.

It was a clear night and there were countless stars. I inhaled the pleasantly cool air and looked at my husband. Carter let his hand drop away.

"I miss this place," he said.

"Did I drive you away?"

"No, I've stayed away by choice."

"It's all so sad," I said, staring off down the dark valley. "I think we're a tragic pair. People shouldn't be as unhappy as we seem to be."

"You're talking about the past. Amnesiacs aren't supposed to do that, my dear."

I smiled at his teasing.

"I'm learning all about myself, about us, very quickly."

"I wonder if you're better off not knowing," he said, a trace of sadness in his voice.

"I can't run away from who I am," I replied.

"No, I suppose you can't."

"You'd like for me to change, though, wouldn't you?"

"What difference does it make? Your condition is temporary. It's probably better in the long run to treat you as the person I know you to be."

His words seemed cruel—or at least unkind—though what he was saying was not only obvious, it was also reasonable. Why should he assume the burden of my sins? I sighed and looked away.

"I'd like to believe in you, Hillary," he said. "But it isn't as simple as just giving you the benefit of the doubt."

"If I could erase the past, I would." My eyes shimmered. "But even if you were willing, *they* wouldn't let me."

Carter knew whom I was referring to. "They" were the police, and "they" were coming for me in the morning, though their purpose was still somewhat vague. "They" were the whole issue, it seemed to me—maybe the final arbiter of who I really was. My past not only defined me, it was my destiny.

"I don't think you should jump to any conclusions," he said. "Let's wait and see what they have to say."

He reached out and took my bare arms, seemingly to savor the feel of my skin. His hands were quite warm, and he gripped me firmly as he searched my eyes. I was sure then that he had brought me to the terrace to touch me, to connect with me physically. He had wanted to be close to me. And maybe I'd come along because I wanted to be close to him.

There were signs of desire in Carter's eyes. Heat. My heart picked up its beat when he lowered his mouth toward mine. His kiss was tender and it aroused me. I'd hungered for this—for the affirmation, for the affection—more than I knew. But still I wasn't prepared for it. I didn't expect to want him as much as I did.

I kissed Carter every bit as deeply as he kissed me. Then, at exactly the same moment, we pulled apart, retreating as swiftly as we'd come together. When I looked into his eyes I saw the reflection of my own feelings—the same doubt, distrust, and fear that I myself felt.

And when he released me, I realized that the issues separating us remained unresolved. The past, like the future, was undeniable. The morning would come. It would come much too soon.

WHERE DOLPHINS GO
by
PEGGY WEBB

"Ms. Webb has an inventive mind brimming
with originality that makes all of her books
special reading."
—*Romantic Times*

*To Susan Riley, the dolphins at the Oceanfront Research Center
were her last chance to reach her frail, broken child. Yet when she
brought Jeffy to the Center, she never expected to have to contend
with a prickly doctor who made it clear that he didn't intend to
get involved. Quiet, handsome, and hostile, Paul Taylor was a
wounded man, and when Susan learned of the tragedy behind his
anguish, she knew she had to help. But what began as compassion
soon turned to desire, and now Susan was falling for a man who
belonged to someone else. . . .*

"A woman came to see me today," Bill said. "A woman and
a little boy."

Paul went very still.

"Her name is Susan . . . Susan Riley. She knew about the
center from that article in the newspaper last week."

There had been many articles written about Dr. Bill
McKenzie and the research he did with dolphins. The most
recent one, though, had delved into the personality of the
dolphins themselves. An enterprising reporter had done his
homework. "Dolphins," he had written, "relate well to people. Some even seem to have extrasensory perception. They
seem to sense when a person is sick or hurt or depressed."

"Her little boy has a condition called truncus arteriosus . . ." Bill squinted in the way he always did when he
was judging a person's reaction.

Paul was careful not to show one. *Truncus arteriosus. A condition of the heart. Malfunctioning arteries. Surgery required.*

"Bill, I don't practice medicine anymore."

"I'm not asking you to practice medicine. I'm asking you to listen."

"I'm listening."

"The boy was scheduled for surgery, but he had a stroke before it could be performed."

For God's sake, Paul. Do something. DO SOMETHING!

"Bill . . ."

"The child is depressed, doesn't respond to anything, anybody. She thought the dolphins might be the answer. She wanted to bring him here on a regular basis."

"You told her no, of course."

"I'm a marine biologist, not a psychologist." Bill slumped in his chair. "I told her no."

"The child needs therapy, not dolphins."

"That's what I thought, but now . . ." Bill gave Paul that squinty-eyed look. "You're a doctor, Paul. Maybe if I let her bring the boy here during feeding times—"

"No. Dammit, Bill. Look at me. I can't even help myself, let alone a dying child and a desperate mother."

Bill looked down at his shoes and counted to ten under his breath. When he looked up Paul could see the pity in his eyes.

He hated that most of all. . . .

Susan hadn't meant to cry.

She knew before she came to the Oceanfront Research Center that her chances of success were slim. And yet she had to try. She couldn't live with herself if she didn't do everything in her power to help Jeffy.

Her face was already wet with tears as she lifted her child from his stroller and placed him in the car. He was so lifeless, almost as if he had already died and had forgotten to take his body with him. When she bent over him to fasten the seat belt, her tears dripped onto his still face.

He didn't even notice.

She swiped at her tears, mad at herself. Crying wasn't going to help Jeffy. Crying wasn't going to help either of them.

Resolutely she folded the stroller and put it in the backseat. Then she blew her nose and climbed into the driver's seat. Couldn't let Jeffy know she was sad. Did he see? Did he know?

The doctors had assured her that he did. That the stroke damage had been confined to areas of the brain that affected his motor control. That his bright little mind and his personality were untouched. And yet, he sat beside her like some discarded rag doll, staring at nothing.

Fighting hard against the helpless feeling she sometimes got when she looked at Jeffy, she turned the key in the ignition and waited for the old engine to warm up. She was not helpless. And she refused to let herself become that way.

"Remember that little song you love so much, Jeffy? The one Mommy wrote?" Jeffy stared at his small sneakers.

Sweat plastered Susan's hair to the sides of her face and made the back of her sundress stick to the seat.

"Mommy's going to sing it to you, darling, while we drive." She put the car into gear and backed out of the parking space, giving herself time to get the quiver out of her voice. She was *not* going to cry again. "You remember the words, don't you, sweetheart? Help Mommy sing, Jeffy."

" 'Sing with a voice of gladness; sing with a voice of joy.'" Susan's voice was neither glad nor joyful, but at least it no longer quivered. Control was easier in the daytime. It was at night, lying in the dark all by herself, when she lost it. She had cried herself to sleep many nights, muffling the sounds in the pillow in case Jeffy, sleeping in the next room, could hear.

" 'Shout for the times of goodness.' " How many good times could Jeffy remember? " 'Shout for the time of cheer.' " How many happy times had he had? Born with a heart condition, he had missed the ordinary joys other children took for granted—chasing a dog, kicking a ball, tumbling in the leaves, outrunning the wind.

" 'Sing with a voice that's hopeful . . . ' " Susan sang on, determined to be brave, determined to bring her child back from that dark, silent world he had entered.

As the car took a curve, Jeffy's head lolled to the side so he was staring straight at her. All the brightness of childhood that should be in his eyes was dulled over by four years of pain and defeat.

Why do you let me hurt?

The message in those eyes made her heart break.

The song died on her lips, the last clear notes lingering in the car like a party guest who didn't know it was time to go home. Susan turned her head to look out the window.

Biloxi was parching under the late afternoon sun. Dust devils shimmered in the streets. Palm trees, sagging and dusty, looked as tired as she felt. It seemed years since she had had a peaceful night's sleep. An eternity since she had had a day of fun and relaxation.

She was selfish to the core. Thinking about her own needs, her own desires. She had to think about Jeffy. There must be something that would spark his interest besides the dolphins.

And don't miss these heart-stopping romances from Bantam Books, on sale in January

THE BELOVED SCOUNDREL
by the nationally bestselling author
Iris Johansen
"You'll be riveted from beginning to end as [Iris Johansen] holds you captive to a love story of grand proportions."
—*Romantic Times* on
The Magnificent Rogue

VIXEN
by **Jane Feather**
A passionate tale of an iron-willed nobleman who suddenly becomes the guardian of a mischievous, orphaned beauty.

ONE FINE DAY
by **Theresa Weir**
"Theresa Weir's writing is poignant, passionate and powerful. *One Fine Day* delivers intense emotion and compelling characters that will capture the hearts of readers."
—*New York Times* bestselling author Jayne Ann Krentz

CALL JAN SPILLER'S ASTROLINE

OFFICIAL RULES

To enter the sweepstakes below carefully follow all instructions found elsewhere in this offer.

The **Winners Classic** will award prizes with the following approximate maximum values: 1 Grand Prize: $26,500 (or $25,000 cash alternate); 1 First Prize: $3,000; 5 Second Prizes: $400 each; 35 Third Prizes: $100 each; 1,000 Fourth Prizes: $7.50 each. Total maximum retail value of Winners Classic Sweepstakes is $42,500. Some presentations of this sweepstakes may contain individual entry numbers corresponding to one or more of the aforementioned prize levels. To determine the Winners, individual entry numbers will first be compared with the winning numbers preselected by computer. For winning numbers not returned, prizes will be awarded in random drawings from among all eligible entries received. Prize choices may be offered at various levels. If a winner chooses an automobile prize, all license and registration fees, taxes, destination charges and, other expenses not offered herein are the responsibility of the winner. If a winner chooses a trip, travel must be complete within one year from the time the prize is awarded. Minors must be accompanied by an adult. Travel companion(s) must also sign release of liability. Trips are subject to space and departure availability. Certain black-out dates may apply.

The following applies to the sweepstakes named above:

No purchase necessary. You can also enter the sweepstakes by sending your name and address to: P.O. Box 508, Gibbstown, N.J. 08027. Mail each entry separately. Sweepstakes begins 6/1/93. Entries must be received by 12/30/94. Not responsible for lost, late, damaged, misdirected, illegible or postage due mail. Mechanically reproduced entries are not eligible. All entries become property of the sponsor and will not be returned.

Prize Selection/Validations: Selection of winners will be conducted no later than 5:00 PM on January 28, 1995, by an independent judging organization whose decisions are final. Random drawings will be held at 1211 Avenue of the Americas, New York, N.Y. 10036. Entrants need not be present to win. Odds of winning are determined by total number of entries received. Circulation of this sweepstakes is estimated not to exceed 200 million. All prizes are guaranteed to be awarded and delivered to winners. Winners will be notified by mail and may be required to complete an affidavit of eligibility and release of liability which must be returned within 14 days of date on notification or alternate winners will be selected in a random drawing. Any prize notification letter or any prize returned to a participating sponsor, Bantam Doubleday Dell Publishing Group, Inc., its participating divisions or subsidiaries, or the independent judging organization as undeliverable will be awarded to an alternate winner. Prizes are not transferable. No substitution for prizes except as offered or as may be necessary due to unavailability, in which case a prize of equal or greater value will be awarded. Prizes will be awarded approximately 90 days after the drawing. All taxes are the sole responsibility of the winners. Entry constitutes permission (except where prohibited by law) to use winners' names, hometowns, and likenesses for publicity purposes without further or other compensation. Prizes won by minors will be awarded in the name of parent or legal guardian.

Participation: Sweepstakes open to residents of the United States and Canada, except for the province of Quebec. Sweepstakes sponsored by Bantam Doubleday Dell Publishing Group, Inc., (BDD), 1540 Broadway, New York, NY 10036. Versions of this sweepstakes with different graphics and prize choices will be offered in conjunction with various solicitations or promotions by different subsidiaries and divisions of BDD. Where applicable, winners will have their choice of any prize offered at level won. Employees of BDD, its divisions, subsidiaries, advertising agencies, independent judging organization, and their immediate family members are not eligible.

Canadian residents, in order to win, must first correctly answer a time limited arithmetical skill testing question. Void in Puerto Rico, Quebec and wherever prohibited or restricted by law. Subject to all federal, state, local and provincial laws and regulations. For a list of major prize winners (available after 1/29/95): send a self-addressed, stamped envelope entirely separate from your entry to: Sweepstakes Winners, P.O. Box 517, Gibbstown, NJ 08027. Requests must be received by 12/30/94. DO NOT SEND ANY OTHER CORRESPONDENCE TO THIS P.O. BOX.